THE VANISHING ACT

Prawin Adhikari lives in Kathmandu, where he teaches and writes fiction and screenplays. He has translated *A Land of Our Own* by Suvash Darnal and a collection of short stories, *Chapters*, by Amod Bhattarai. He has also written a couple of feature films in Nepali. Prawin is an assistant editor at *La.Lit*, the literary magazine.

THE VANISHING ACT

STORIES

Prawin Adhikari

RUPA

Published by
Rupa Publications India Pvt. Ltd 2014
7/16, Ansari Road, Daryaganj
New Delhi 110002

Sales centres:
Allahabad Bengaluru Chennai
Hyderabad Jaipur Kathmandu
Kolkata Mumbai

ISBN: 978-81-291-2431-9

10 9 8 7 6 5 4 3 2 1

First impression 2014

Typeset in Adobe Jenson Pro by SÜRYA, New Delhi

CONTENTS

THE BOY FROM BANAUTI

Grandfather would read one book here and another scroll there through the year, but only in November—after consulting his astrological chart—would he spread the contents of his father's old almirah in the palliative sun to drive the moisture and must out and to renew the mild poison in the hemlock that yellowed the pages. It was also the day of the year when we, the children of the extended family, were reminded of how much there is to learn, how much there is to inherit by way of words. Great-grandfather had collected or written with his own hand all of these obscure or pedestrian Sanskrit texts, boiling black angeri berries for the ink, sharpening nibs from bamboo and reed (because a quill, which originates in flesh, would have been profane), splitting bamboo to collect the thin film within to layer into paper. I hated the sight. It was a taunt, I knew it even then; I knew it was meant to burden the youngest boys in the family with guilt for not following the family trade, for packing their bags and going to an English-medium school instead of learning Sanskrit.

I hated that I was expected to learn, to memorize, to know. To remember details, causes and consequences, descriptions and explanations, names, genealogies, salutations and shortcuts to salvation. Examine the back of my head and you'll see scars from falling from heights, or objects falling on my head from heights: roofs, branches, low bluffs along a stream, low walls, high walls. It is a miracle that I can remember anything at all. Yet, on such days in November, I was expected to kneel by Grandfather's side and examine the past that my generation was meant to inherit: prayers, puran, commentaries and poetry. On such days, my schoolbag seemed extra heavy, doubly annoying.

'Come here,' Grandfather called me on that particular day and made me take off my shoes before I could kneel on the straw mat and yak-hair blanket on which he sat. 'Read this English,' he said.

It was dated March, 1915. A dedication to Great-grandfather, in a neat hand, written by the Chief Engineer, Allahabad Bridge, Allahabad, on the title page of a handsomely produced copy of the *Amarkosh*, a thesaurus of Sanskrit. Grandfather smiled. I couldn't tell what he seemed more satisfied by: his father's adventures or his grandson's ability to read letters with a third-grade education. I hastily slipped on my shoes, picked up my bag and walked away.

School was a mile away in the bazaar. A handful of us walked from our neighbourhood in Panchayat Bhavan to the bazaar every day. It was easier to walk along the highway, but Mother considered it too dangerous: each year, dozens died in motor accidents on the dirt shoulders of the highway. She thought everything was designed to kill her youngest child: trees, ponds, rivers, lorries and buses, wasps and hornets, berries, foreigners. So we walked through paddies laid bare after the harvest, dotted with stubble, dew-mulched and yielding underfoot. We jumped nimbly over muddy irrigation ditches and raced between fodder trees or houses along the way. Malla's steam-engine rice mill announced nine o'clock with puffs of black smoke and a toot-toot-toot. That was our signal to run to school, racing to be the first to cross the mill-yard, to be the first to cross the highway to Gorkha, be the first to jump through the gates at Sun Shine English Medium.

But on that day, I didn't want to run; I didn't want to reach the school where each day I was punished during the morning assemblies in the yard—for forgetting the national anthem when it was my turn to lead the school, for nails hastily chewed down just before inspection, for reading Surendra Mohan Pathak thrillers in Hindi or smuggling in Nagraj comics for the boys who lived in the hostel. I didn't want to face Mr Hansen from Goa, who taught social sciences and loved to pick on Rajendra, Bir Bahadur and me for not doing our homework. I ran ahead, slipped behind a hedge near my cousin Ishwor's house, and crouched to urinate as my friends walked past. They must have thought I had raced on, trying to breach the school gates before the nine-fifteen bell rang, before the principal's brother Amshu fetched his cane to whip the latecomers.

After rolling my socks into tidy balls to stuff into my shoes, stuffing the shoes into the school bag and burying the bag under banana-leaf mulch by the guava tree behind Ishwor's home, I sniffed the air and smiled to the sun. What a day! A clear sky, the sun mild on the skin, shades cold as they ought to be in November, and six whole hours languidly spread before me.

I wandered aimlessly, ducking to hide from elders who might know me or my parents or my teachers, stealing through kitchen gardens, crouching to watch buffalos tethered to stakes to soak in the sun, letting cactus thorns scratch the shin that itched, picking, sniffing at, and then flinging away, a dead bluebird. I wandered to escape rote and recital, to inspect closely how spit forces touch-me-nots to fold and to hide from the foliage long enough to fool it into unfolding, run a finger along the saw-edge of waxy pineapple leaves, pick beetles from cow-patties, squeeze between bamboos to squat on new shoots, eat wild kauso seeds and dig for fern roots, listen to the hoots of owls that perch on jackfruit trees and don't sleep, chase the howls of sly jackals that haunt the edge of the forest, forget lessons in arithmetic of yesterday, the past week, the entire year.

Ram Shah Madhyamik was quiet for the time of the

morning. I marched right through the school grounds, in
through the west gate, out through the east. None of the
teachers who came to their doors tried to stop me. This
wasn't my school, these weren't my tyrants. Here and now,
I could walk unmolested by authority. What a world!

Then it was past the jalebi shop with the soot-faced boy,
past Arjun's mother's hut, down the crumbling chalk-hill
behind Koirala's Veterinary and Agriculture Shop that
always smelled of poison, but on its board showed seeds
and an egg and a hen and a cow all of the same size, life
growing outwards, out to the downhill road to Gorkha, all
the way to where the bridge across Marshyangdi stretched
a full hundred metres, a crawl along the rails, spitting over
the side, measuring the arc the wind made with the glob of
spit before it became one with the river's foam, letting the
river reel in my head, stepping back just in time to say,
'Wah! Marshyangdi almost sucked me down!'

Daraundi met Marshyangdi by a corner stained with
charcoal-strewn pits. Even during the day, even from afar,
the corner had a strong, tidal pull, like being sucked into a
separate world. The crippled babaji in the Shiva temple
was awake, unusually early for him: it was common
knowledge he dived to the depths of the rivers during the
night to collect human bones, breaking the churned surface
of the waters with his withered, shrivelled arm. He sat
combing his long hair with his one good hand, fanning its
oily grey length over one knee, out over the stone threshold
of the small, squat temple. Like always, he called me with

the shrivelled arm he normally kept in its wooden box, pointing up to the Sun God to whom he had offered the limb many years ago.

I ran down the chalky path to the river that curved along the base of the bluff with the Shiva temple. Daraundi carved pockets of still water or shallow pools where long beards of algae and clear pebbly floors alternated. If the sun lasted an entire day the shallow pools would become warmer than the snow-fed currents of the river. By my favourite wading spot was Pushpa, an equal delinquent, sitting on the reddest, smoothest rock. He wasn't wearing his uniform. When he saw me, he came bounding over rocks, leaping over the kids in the wading pool. We shook hands like men: Pushpa stark naked, me in my Friday uniform. He led me back to the rock where he was cooking his crayfish caught in the paddies by the river. Pushpa's catch was impressive: thirteen, plump, sun-roasted to a pink hue, soon curling to sniff their tails like dogs, soon crunchy and sweet. Pushpa leaped from rock to rock to the bush where his clothes sat under a stone, and I surveyed the world.

It was the usual crowd of truants. Shankar, Binod, Sujan, Kishor, Kumar, Omkaji, Amrit, Rupesh and Sudip Malla were diving and swimming. Sujan was only a year older than me, but he could swim clear across Marshyangdi during the floods, without getting a hair on his head wet, never once cutting his arms out of the river, jumping near Dadim Dhik near Ram Shah Madhyamik, floating all the way across as easily as if he were strolling through a wide meadow. I couldn't swim, and most of the boys were my uncles from my mother's side, an entire village of cousins and second cousins, who would gladly beat me up at any excuse they found. Mother would take their side, too— she'd interrogate me on why I was wherever I happened to be apprehended by one of those thugs. So I sat on Pushpa's red rock until he called me to Hari-Hara.

Hari-Hara were two rocks, each the size of Bagaley Ba's smaller teashop near Narayan Malla's rice mill. Where they leaned into each other they made a short tunnel with a cold heart. Pushpa lit the cigarette he had brought for me. He pulled at it, puffed his cheeks out, and exhaled with a convulsive gathering of the chest and stomach. I took the cigarette. I didn't smoke it right away. I scratched the tip of my nose with my thumb, but didn't put the cigarette in my mouth. I spat through the gap in my teeth and rubbed the spit into the sand with the big toe. I whistled a little. I then pulled at the cigarette and held my breath.

It felt like I had gathered all the dry leaves around the bamboo grove in Kunduley, all the brambles between Narighat and Khanikhola, all of last year's mustard stalks after harvest and lit a fire somewhere under my throat, above my stomach. My chest heaved; pellets of air hit my ears from the inside. Something like a snort or a giggle or a belch or a sneeze or a cry escaped from a corner of my mouth. I exhaled. The smoke had gone thin and black.

'Good!' I said as Pushpa puffed up his cheeks to keep the smoke captive. He opened his mouth, letting curlicues of smoke rise on their own. Pushpa pinched the cigarette, wrapped it in a syaula leaf and put it away. He made a whooping yell and jumped into the wading pool. Syankanchha and Rakesh and Keshav and Marichey and Gajaley's son waited for Pushpa to finish splashing around before dipping themselves up to the chin and thrashing with their legs.

I was still seeing tiny sparks of light—stars—just around my eyes, the part of life that is usually grey and invisible. Pushpa's stone felt too hot. I slid down the length of its smooth face, still wearing my uniform, and splashed into the pool. I slept in the water, looking up at the boys who came close to yell and laugh until another distraction took them away. I really could hold my breath: nothing seemed distinct, not even my hands, and any pebble held before my eyes seemed round and shiny and money-like. Riches. When I sat up, sputtering the little water that had gone in through the nose, gasping for air, I saw the boy from Banauti pointing, laughing at me.

Although he pointed at me, nobody else was looking. He laughed soundlessly, without a pip or a squeak. His head was shorn, perhaps because of the sores and scabs that mottled his scalp. He was related to me, if you drew a line that wormed six generations back and wormed forward again until it tied me to him. Properly, the boy from Banauti was an uncle from my father's side. His blind father sat outside their house to sell yogurt and walking sticks to people from Kathmandu trying to climb to Manakamana.

His sister had thrown herself from the suspension bridge over Marshyangdi the day her friends told her that she had failed her SLC exams. Her friends had been joking, trying to scare her. She never got to know. The boy from Banauti now lived with Keshav's family, away from his blind father who still milked the buffaloes and polished walking sticks in his spare time, but also cried and cursed in angry fits, swinging his sickle and stick at anything that moved, until the foaming spit dried to salt and tore open the skin of his mouth.

'Why are you laughing?' I said. I knew why he laughed. He thought I had done something funny.

'You're wet! Everything is wet!' he said.

'You're in the water. You're wet, too,' I said.

'That is your school uniform,' he said. 'Your mother will be angry.'

'And you don't even have a mother,' I said. I plugged both ears with my fingers and plunged my head underwater. Small, slow bubbles through the nose. Continuous. Hold your breath until you are sitting upright. Wipe your face with your palms before exhaling. The boy from Banauti raised his head to look at me before concentrating on his hands. His lips and brows twitched.

'And your father is blind,' I said. He didn't look up. I knew I would next tell him that his sister threw herself from the bridge. There was nothing else left to throw at him. Sujan was jumping on Kishor's shoulders, trying to keep him in the water, while Shankar was pulling Sujan's leg. The wading pool was still because everyone had chosen a rock each and was warming their ears to bring the water out. It is easy. Find a large, sun-cooked rock. Embrace it, facedown, with your ear glued to it. Close your eyes, and drift into warm, sticky dreams.

The boy from Banauti looked up. His chin quivered and the large, dirty-brown eyes turned wet and trembled. I sat by him. 'What are you doing?' I asked.

'Nests,' he said, 'swallows' nests.' He dug into the wet sand until water seeped from all sides into the rut. He dipped his palm, let the wetness run down to the fingertips and drip: solid, wet beads of sand. He arranged the beads, every drop placed with deliberation. Streets. Spires. Hedges. A temple with a dome that rose in two concentric spirals, like the domes in the books which the Singapore Lahure kids brought to school. He stopped and pointed at my hands.

I scooped water and sand, but my beads fell in uneven sizes. The boy from Banauti laughed at first. I drew outlines on the sand for the layout of my village, patted down sand for the foundations, then started over. Now the boy from Banauti watched intently, added his own drops to augment, once using a crooked finger to scoop and transplant a bead to perfect effect, changing a hut to a sentry-box by piling up a pyramid of cannonballs on the roof. Then he started laughing. I laughed with him.

'Who works here?' He pointed to the newly finished sentry-box.

'I don't know,' I said, 'it is a sentry-box.'

'I know what it is,' he said. He was annoyed. 'I said, Who works here?'

It is a stupid lump of stupid wet sand, I wanted to say. Everybody else was busy shouting or jumping. Pushpa and Sujan appeared by Hari-Hara. Sujan tried to blow smoke rings. Sujan could do anything a grown-up could. 'I said, Who works here?' The boy from Banauti brought a finger too close to my sentry-box with the cannonballs on the roof.

You have to know. That is the whole point. Knowing. Exactly. Who, where, what, when. That is the point. Why. That is the point also. Otherwise you are just a stupid kid playing with wet sand. Just a stupid kid.

The boy from Banauti was raving now. I tried to imagine his blind father's rage. The last time we climbed to Manakamana, Mother had taken me to their home and had made me eat yogurt prepared by his father. The old man had insisted upon reading my fortune. His coarse fingers attentively hovered over the thin lines of my palms. He said good things. Then he cried. He said, 'I wish my son had half the good fortune you have.' He took my face in his hands, gingerly rubbed my forehead, said I had a wide forehead, one for fortune and fame.

The boy from Banauti knew—exactly who, where, what, when. Even the why. He was becoming more and more agitated. He had a name for each intersection of each neighbourhood, each face of the temple, the person sitting or absent from each window, everything being sold by each vendor in each derelict corner behind large warehouses. His was not a village, but a city, with a park where the king's younger son played with his vast army of retainers while the king did what? Hold jousts and chases to find an eligible prince for his daughter. Anybody speaking calmly would need a year to finish inventing and detailing everything the boy from Banauti knew and jabbered on and on about, but it took him less time than it took for me to work up a temper.

I kicked sand into his face. The stupid wet sand he had been playing with. I trampled down his vast city. I killed the sentry in my own sentry-box with the cannonballs on the roof. The sentry poked his head out of the tiny window, dull bayonet leading, trying to prop my foot up with a pin-prick. Then I kicked the double-spiralled temple to the face of the boy from Banauti. Although he sat there dumbstruck, his chin quivering, one hand on his throat to either stifle a scream or to bottle his breath, I knew he knew the where, when, who, how. I was the marauding why. I spread my arms wide, faced the sky and laughed maniacally.

I quickly picked one of Pushpa's shrivelled crayfish and chewed on it. Another. The boy from Banauti walked away. 'I'll tell your mother,' he said before disappearing behind a rock.

❧

I left my clothes behind Pushpa's rock and admired my toes peeking out of the water. I slipped underwater and blew bubbles, holding each pearl of air at the cusp of my mouth, watching it pull its shape from within me, then leave me to rush against the sky. None of the boys had returned into the pool when I sat up to breathe. Back underwater, to the place where everything was indistinct and looked like bright coins. Blue and black and beige and white pebbles like coins. There is a country somewhere in the middle of the Pacific, a place which *Yuva Manch Monthly* writes 'Did you know?' facts about, where these pebbles are riches, precious as diamonds and malachite. Malachite. The World Cup is made of gold and malachite. Did you know?

Somebody grabbed my hair and lifted me out of the water. It was Binod, Shankar's twin.

'What did I do?' I screamed at him. He looked at me, puzzled, but didn't let go of my hair. I had to use my knees to stand. Pebbles and coarse sand scraped my kneecaps.

'Don't sit like that in the water, you ass,' he said, 'I thought you were drowning. That you'd drowned.'

'I can hold my breath,' I said. He grabbed me by the nape and threw me to the bank.

'Don't go back into the water,' he said. Nobody else was around. He climbed Pushpa's rock. I climbed after him. One roasted crayfish fell into the river when my wet toes nudged it loose. A line of pale naked buttocks jumped from rock to rock, running downriver to where Daraundi met

Marshyangdi. Babaji screamed from the temple, running from one corner to another, his atrophied hand still pointing to the gods.

'What happened?' I asked. Binod put a hand on my shoulder and rubbed the nape he had roughed but a moment ago.

Sujan and Shankar bobbed over Daraundi's water, racing fast towards Marshyangdi. Daraundi brought clear water, fed by glaciers, or mountain springs filtered through thousands of paddies, while Marshyangdi descended furiously, intent upon grinding together the rocks in her belly. Where Daraundi met Marshyangdi, Daraundi recoiled. Sujan was thrown back by that recoil. Shankar dived into the seam and came up for air thirty paces downstream. Everybody else ran along the river, shouting, screaming. A line of people stood on the suspension bridge and pointed this way and that, made noises that didn't carry to where we stood. My toe slipped an inch and I lurched slightly; Binod caught me by my arm and steadied me on the rock without taking his eyes off Sujan and Shankar.

'What is his name?' Binod asked. Whose? 'The boy. You were making swallows' nests with him. The boy from Banauti.'

'He is my relative,' I said. I didn't know his name.

'He fell,' Binod said.

Sujan and Shankar could be seen, diving, coming to the surface, riding the white water of the rivers to propel them to the whirlpools that swallowed bodies. Amrit and Omkaji shouted to Sujan and Shankar. Sujan dived once more, but Shankar came to the bank. He floated on his back in a corner, one hand grabbing the rock behind him. Sujan finally climbed out of the water, but stranded himself between two granite ledges with water on either side. He crawled to a narrow bar of sand and hid his face in his hands.

Pushpa climbed his rock and teetered with one hand on my shoulder. He brushed off the remaining crayfish into the river.

'What was his name?' Binod asked Pushpa, who shook his head.

'We should have asked,' Binod said sombrely. He put his hand on my shoulder and rubbed my neck. 'Go home,' he said. 'Go home, but don't talk about this. Don't mention you were here.'

Pushpa and I buttoned our shirts in silence. I hadn't yet learned how to tie shoelaces quickly. It took me a while. Up the hill, in the temple, Babaji was locking his arm into a wooden box suspended from the roof. 'Go home,' he said perfunctorily. Pushpa threw away what remained of the cigarette, still wrapped in the syaula leaf. I wanted to stand on the edge of the bluff and read the rivers in both directions, as far as my eyes could see. Who knows when the boy from Banauti will call for help, I thought. But it felt like it had been a very long day. The most recent minutes were interminable, like the yarn on my mute uncle Madhav's dhaka loom, looping around something not very far, anchored to the weight inside, and each thread returning, over and over, to the same place, just a slightly different spot.

Pilgrims on the suspension bridge continued to peer into the current long after it made any sense for them to. What a day! Not even noon yet, the sun still mild and pale, and a boy disappeared even as dozens of people watched. Six generations ago, there had been a man who worked in the jungles along these very rivers, tended to his cows, gathered fodder and firewood, and read fortunes for a small fee. From him came hundreds, including Grandfather who sunned his yellowed pages of scriptures while his distant cousin groped blindly at the air in Banauti for his son's return; from the first astrologer came the sister who jumped into the river, and from him came I: truant, delinquent, ignorant. I knew nothing of those who had passed before me. There was one who could have known, who could have conjured their faces and voices through an act of will and invention, but the river took him before I could ask his name, before I could ask him how his mother had died, or if he remembered her at all. And it made me melancholy to understand that I didn't know enough about the boy from Banauti, or about myself.

MAYAPURI

I haven't returned to Khaireni in twelve years. I have passed through the town, dismayed each time by how much the landscape has changed, but I haven't stopped to call on old friends and relatives. Mother likes to repeat to me what her friends say when she visits the old house in Khaireni. Her visits revolve around the planting and harvesting of rice, except when the routine is punctuated by the death of her elders; so the missives sent my way by women who remember me as a child are mostly cheerful and full of fondness.

But time has erased the contours of the life I remember from my childhood. The transformation of Khaireni from a sleepy village into a town began with the construction of the sixty-nine megawatt hydro-electricity project in the late-eighties. Thousands of people and otherworldly machines descended into the narrow valley to dam the Marshyangdi at Markichowk. A tunnel bore right through the base of the Chimkeshwori Mountain, emerging to the

east eleven kilometres later to gain a vertical height of
nearly a hundred metres. The tunnel was large enough for a
truck to rumble through, carrying dynamite sticks and
helmeted labourers from all over South Asia. These trucks
raced between the two ends of the tunnel, passing through
Khaireni, Dhabtar and Markichowk, raising billows of
death-bringing dust that settled on every surface: leaves,
eaves, sills, pots, the million folds in a grandmother's lungs.

At the time of its construction, with its promise of sixty-
nine megawatts, the dam on Marshyangdi was the largest
hydro-electricity project in Nepal. Engineers and technicians
came from all around the world—China, Germany, Japan,
the United States. A fenced-in camp was set up for them
and their families—there was a swimming pool, a school,
gyms and a supermarket, air-conditioning and a borrowing
library, a sealed First World bubble ringed by dung-scented
Third World fields. But the labourers crammed into
whatever rooms they could find in the small village, sleeping
three, four men to a room, and sometimes three men taking
turns to use the same bed in eight-hour stretches. Only
those who arrived in Khaireni with a family—wife,
children—sought more secure boarding.

One such couple rented a one-room wooden shack thrown
together at the edge of our kitchen-garden. Mother liked
the new bride, even though she had eloped against her

father's wish. On evenings when Mother and my aunts spent the hour after dinner rolling cotton wicks or making platters out of saal leaves, the new bride would stay and work with them until her husband hollered for her. I no longer remember their faces or names, but the precious afternoons they stole to fall asleep together between his shifts as a drill operator at the big dam stay with me.

On Sundays—when I didn't have to be in school but none of my friends were around because they studied at the government school—I'd loiter around our house until the heat of high noon put everything and everybody to sleep. I liked stealing to the damp, cold corner behind the new bride's window. I sometimes squatted against the wall with closed eyes to listen, sometimes peeped over the windowsill to watch her sleep. When she stirred, I held my breath.

She was much older than me, but that was only because I was a boy all of ten, my crooked mouth full of a jumble of new and milk teeth. I can't guess how much older she was—she was young, with clear skin and a voice rarely absent of its silky laugh, but she was a woman old enough to have eloped with her man, old enough to play wife. Mother didn't like me to eat in the kitchens of people who rented from us. But if I appeared at the woman's door late in the morning, she'd call me inside, boil a cup of milk for me and ask me to sit quietly. She'd go about her kitchen chores; cutting, cooking, cleaning, looking up occasionally to smile at me, the down over her mouth glistening with sweat. I'd sit on the bed, leafing through her husband's copies of *Manorama* and *Satyakatha*. If the wood fire got too smoky, I'd take the short length of bamboo from her and gently blow at the embers until they turned a hot orange and suddenly erupt, lapping with bright tongues. She'd lean back, wipe the sweat from her face and neck and, with the same hand, tousle my short hair. Or she'd push my shoulder, tipping me over.

Their home was a modest, soot-licked room: a stack of *Mayapuri* and other Bollywood gossip magazines by the bed, two lines stretched along the far wall for clothes, dishes stacked neatly on a plank propped on bricks, a window by the bed with a view of Grandfather's mustard fields. The bed was always neatly made; two soft pillows, a thin quilt folded across the foot of the bed, Hong Kong cotton sheets with flowers or coloured squares. Nailed to the wall were two framed photos: one of him straddling a motorbike clearly set on its stand. The other showed him seated before a mural of a Mughal garden—one of the choice backdrops offered at Annapurna Photo Studio in Khaireni Bazaar—with her sitting awkwardly on his lap. The ceiling and the walls were plastered with pictures of Indian actresses cut out of gossip magazines: Amrita Singh, Poonam Dhillon, Tina Munim, Jaya Prada, Neelam, Sonam, Madhuri, Sridevi. Kimi Katkar, whose feline eyes even then made me uneasy. Zeenat Aman, whom everybody in the village called Jina Tamang. The breathtaking Rekha. A dozen avatars of each woman, watching the bed through thickly lined eyes, the inaudible moans from their parted mouths slithering and sliding over the bed like a nest of invisible serpents.

She always splashed water when she walked back from the tap, the copper pot sitting on the jut of her hip sloshing and dripping to the waist. She never asked me to move away from the door so she could enter. She'd just smile and walk in sideways. She would have washed her face and wiped her neck. I'd walk away from her door. She'd shut the door behind me, latch it. Just about then Mother would call me, or I would walk home, knowing that the woman would be preparing herself in her shack, combing her hair, lining her eyes, stripping to get into a washed Singapore sarong and a loose shirt. After eating, I'd wait for everybody to busy themselves before climbing the guava tree by her window, waiting for her husband to jump down from a truck.

Like a practiced thief, I would skulk to my corner behind their windows and listen to the silent sound of their eating. The man would perhaps not take his eyes off the mound of rice and dal before him, biting into a green chili or onion, while she hugged her knees to her chest, the ladle on the ready by her side. He'd step out of the door to wash his hand, she'd take his plate and start by eating his leftovers. He'd return, throw his bulk on the bed, making it creak for the first time in the afternoon, followed soon by another creak of her sitting on the bed. She'd stroke his forehead, perhaps, or the bulge of his biceps tired from pressing the diamond-tipped drill into unyielding granite before the sappers filled the bore-holes with dynamite.

Perhaps she'd knead his palms with her thumbs while he closed his eyes and smiled contentedly. He'd untie her hair, perhaps grabbing her by the nape and pulling her mouth to his. The world buzzed with the calls of crickets amplified in the bright dazzle of mustard flowers. The roar of the big river would sweep so close that it would lift and soar me away, over the cusp of the eastern mountains. Inside, the neatly made bed would come unmade stitch by stitch, fold by careful fold. The bed would pound against the wooden boards of the wall and jar my head leaning against it. An intense need to urinate would burn inside me. I'd pull my penis out and urinate on my hand, careful not to make any sound, careful not to give away my place in their game. And, quiet. The splash of urine on my thigh would grow cold. I'd peep into the window.

And there she'd be: her hair damp, a hand clamped over his chest, a leg thrown over his waist. They'd slumber, snoring, shuffling together in their sleep like one shape of flesh, asking and yielding even without knowing. He always napped with his arms thrown behind his head, but she clung to him like a thirsty vine biting into a trunk for its sap. Her leg always startled me: the pale slope of the inner thigh, the knob and crook of her knee, the wandering toes. She never kept her leg inside the quilt thrown over their bodies. Sometimes he'd put his hand on her thigh. She'd respond immediately, pressing into him, digging her heel around his leg, breathing through her open mouth.

It would take an entire afternoon of lonely roving through

the village to quiet my anxiety. The fire under the skin would simmer down only when my friends came home from their school and we could start our games of hide-and-seek, or divide the group into Pandava and Kaurava to re-enact the war with dull bamboo arrows shot from rigid, dry bamboo bows, hitting nothing, harming no one, going nowhere.

One Sunday afternoon, she didn't stay home after preparing his lunch. She worried over a bucket of clothes, putting her back into the labour. She didn't answer when he washed himself and teased her by dropping beads of water on her spine. Instead, she furiously kneaded the washing in her red bucket. He gave up, looked up at the guava tree from where I was spying on them, and walked into their shack. She didn't look up even when he came out after ten minutes and sauntered off to the cigarette shop across the road. He smoked without patience, threw the cigarette into the sewer, waved down a lorry and left for his shift in the tunnel deep in the bowels of the mountain. When the lorry went around the corner, she abandoned the washing under the waterspout.

The door was ajar. I pushed it open. Her bamboo comb with fine teeth was stuck in the tangle of her hair; she jerked at it with force to free it. I showed her the bar of laundry soap I had picked from the waterspout. She turned away, perhaps to wipe her eyes, but when she turned back, she was smiling again.

'Will you go with me, Kanchho?' she asked. 'Will you go with me? It has four months since I saw a video.'

'Whose video hall? Kumar Kanchha or Maskey?' I asked. I preferred Maskey's video hall—it was four houses down from my school whereas Kumar Kanchha's video hall was across the alley from the school. I didn't want my teachers to see me sneaking out after watching a film with Mithun Chakraborty or Sanjay Dutt in it. She laughed. 'Nobody will see you, Kanchho,' she said, throwing a dupatta over my head. 'I'll hide you like a little baby,' she said. I pretended to push her away.

'He'll do his homework in the evening,' she told Mother, who was worrying a frayed length of rope hanging from the roof of the cowshed. Mother called me to her, checked my teeth, the grime under the collar and dirt behind the ears.

'He'll cry next week and ask for money to go to the video hall again,' Mother said.

'No, I won't!' I whined. 'Today! Only just today and never ever, ever never again.'

'It'll become a bad habit,' Mother said to her, but I had already started crying, so she pulled me closer, pinched away the snot hanging from my nose, and wiped my face with her sari.

'No, it won't!' I whined, 'Never ever, ever never!'

As we started off, Mother laughed and said, 'He won't let me sleep tonight, not until he tells me the whole story.' She laughed with Mother, put her arm around my shoulder and pulled me along. I held her hand and she swung it. At the Mankamana Fresh Bakery down the road, doughnuts were frying in ghee. She caught my eyes and winked.

It was a good doughnut, golden outside, steaming inside, the spongy bread like the flesh of an exotic fruit. I gobbled down mine, but she daintily pinched at hers and waited for me to finish. She then gave me what remained of her doughnut. I kept chewing the last mouthful, sweetening it with saliva into warm, white milk.

The blackboard outside Maskey's video hall listed the players: Hero—Mithun Chakraborty! Heroine—Anita Raaj! Villains—Amrish Puri! Ranjit! Comedy Characters—Kader Khan! Asrani! Ranjit was always the rapist. More than once in a movie, he would pin down the hero's sister—or even the heroine herself—against a rock in the forest, or a tree by a pond, or on a revolving bed with gaudy covers. He would then pucker up his wet mouth and bring it to the struggling woman's face. She would scream a long 'Nahiiiin!' and the story would move on to another scene. If, subsequently, the woman hanged herself, or jumped into a river, or closed her eyes and stood before an oncoming train, it meant her honour had been robbed by Ranjit.

At Maskey's video hall that afternoon, I was the only boy and she was the only woman. Men waited patiently for Maskey to clean the reading head of the VCR player with a sharp new banknote before he put the tape in. Mithun danced and sang and fought and beat up Ranjit very badly for grabbing Anita Raaj's hand. An uncle I vaguely knew came in after the intermission and squeezed onto the bench, crowding me towards her. She put an arm around my shoulder and pulled me closer. The uncle pressed against her arm and squished my face into her small, warm breast. On the screen, Ranjit cornered Anita Raaj.

I could hear her breathe quicker. She pulled me closer; the smell of her armpit became foggier but sharper. She crossed and uncrossed her legs, fidgeted on the bench, and squirmed away from the men sitting on either side. Ranjit puckered up and brought his mouth closer. His bloodshot eyes and heavy breath weighed her down. Men who would've hooted and clapped limited themselves to small coughs. The rape was quickly over.

She came around that evening and called Mother outside. But Mother was eating in the kitchen, so she called the woman inside. She squatted by the door.

'What is wrong?' Mother asked.

'He is taking night shifts for the week,' she said after a while. She scratched the mud floor with a toe and whispered to her knees. I selected a dry jute stalk and poked at the embers in the hearth, raising flakes of ash.

'And leaving you all alone in that room?' Mother said. Mother never called the woman's home a shack.

'Why don't you sleep here?' Mother suggested. The woman shook her head.

'If you think it is all right,' she pointed at me, 'I would take him.'

'Where will you put him?' Mother asked. 'That floor is too damp for anybody.'

'The bed is big enough,' the woman said.

Mother looked at me with worry. 'He doesn't like sleeping away from home,' Mother said. 'Even when he goes to his mamaghar he runs home in the evening. He won't let you sleep. He kicks in his sleep.'

'Because I play football,' I said. The jute stalk caught fire. I watched the thin blue smoke rise above the hearth and curl towards the soot-bearded rafters.

Mother told her to make sure I'd wash my feet or I might wet the bed. 'If you play with fire after eating, you'll surely wet the bed,' the woman teased. I jumped up in anger and tried to walk out of the kitchen, but the woman grabbed my arm and pulled me to her, held me until I stopped struggling. She hid her mouth in her shawl and laughed. 'No, you won't,' she said, 'you are a big boy.'

She wiped and stacked away the pots, went to the outhouse and came back smelling of soap. I sat at the edge of the bed, rocking softly to the cadences of exotic names in a gossip rag. She sat on the bed to unbraid and brush her hair.

'Move to this side,' she said, pointing to the edge of the bed.

'I want the window,' I said. She grabbed my shirt and shorts and dragged me across. 'You want me to fall off in the night?' I said.

'You won't!' she said, and went to the door to get rid of

the hair she'd balled from the brush. She stood at the threshold, spitting into the hair three times, incanting to it her personal prayers and curses before flinging it into the darkness outside: her greed for the work of women and witches.

By the time she returned from the door, I had wormed back to the window. She approached with a smile dimpling her face, her ten fingers fanned to wiggle and tickle. She dug under my shirt to find the laughing rib and tickled me until I begged for air.

I wanted her to ask me to recount the film we had watched. I wanted to be Mithun, I wanted to be Ranjit. But she pulled me to the nook of her shoulder and flipped through a *Mayapuri*, silently mouthing the gossip, lingering over the pictures. Dharmendra wore very short shorts in a picture as two starlets hung from his thick arms. She pointed at his hairy thighs and laughed.

It was in Mother's bed that I awoke the next day. The woman had returned me after her husband came home before dawn. And so it went for the week—I would run over to her home after dinner and do my homework on the bed as she cleaned up. She'd take me to the waterspout to wash my face, my hands and feet. On Friday night, she said I was beginning to smell ripe enough for a cat to whisk me away. On Saturday, Mother left five rupees with the woman to buy a packet of Wai-Wai noodles for me and took the bus to Dumre to press mustard oil. Although my friends crowded around the waterspout to tease me, and although the woman's husband was home, laughing from his door, the woman made me stand in her red bucket under the waterspout and washed me from the dirty hair to the mucky toes. When she rubbed the soap bar on my buttocks, the boys giggled and ran off. The husband came to the waterspout.

'I come home dirty every day. You never give me a bath,' he said with a smile. The woman's hands turned into vise-grips around my ankle.

'I have to sleep with this one here,' she said and pushed my head under the spout.

I didn't join any of the games my friends played all day that day—they ran to the big river to scour the sandy banks for berries; they raided our orchard across the Khahare stream; they trawled the irrigation ditch along the paddies for fish; they watched Kushal burn down a wasp hive and cook the larvae inside; they ate wild figs and fern roots. But I stayed home, careful to not rub against the walls, careful not to step barefoot on the floor, careful to stay clean for her.

That night, when she came to bed, she smelled my hair and kissed the top of my head. She pulled me to the pillow and said with a tired voice, 'Let's sleep now, Babu.'

But I couldn't sleep. Strange dreams awoke me throughout the night. My breath felt cold on the sheen of sweat covering my arms. A blue field of pale fire spread outside the window; the moonlit mustard fields cascaded all the way to the big river at the edge of the valley. The woman moaned violently and tossed on her back, to her side, her knees clapping, a hand churning the crotch. She moaned again—'No!' She turned away, her damp hair stuck to the pillow, knees clapping again, even more urgently. She arched her back and then threw the quilt to the foot of the bed. An earthy, sharp smell like mushrooms and peach blossoms crushed together fogged around us. When she quivered like a bamboo bow that has just shot a light arrow into the sky, the joints in her spine cracked: she was coming undone, her body was falling apart. I started to sob—I didn't know what was happening to her. She was no longer beautiful but terrifying, grinding her teeth and digging her nails into her thighs. I touched her shoulder to wake her, but she was burning, her shut eyes leaking tears, her breath hot and rank.

She sat up with a start and covered her chest, although she was wearing a shirt. Then she saw her sarong hitched up around her waist, bunched up between her thighs, her hand wet and fragrant. She screamed, jumped out of the bed and searched the corners of the room.

'Where is he?' she demanded. 'Where is he?' She went to the door and tried to pull it open, but it was latched from the inside. I continued to cry, more out of confusion than anything else. She sat on the bed and tried to hide her wet hand in the folds of her sarong. The flush on her face receded, but when she looked up and saw my wide-eyed terror, she blushed. She pulled my head to her chest and kissed it. 'We won't talk about this to anyone, okay,

Kanchho?' she whispered. She wiped my eyes and nose and looked me in the eyes. 'It was a bad dream, Babu, a witch was sitting on my chest,' she said.

Although I pretended to fall asleep, I stayed alert to the sound of her breathing, to the movements of her hands that stroked my neck and wiped her eyes in the dark. There must be something I can do, I thought, something that will make her forget whatever it is that makes her cry.

I didn't wake up at home in the morning, but I heard Mother tell the woman to get me a doughnut from the teashop across the road. Mother wouldn't be home early enough to send me off to school, so she asked the woman to get me ready. I didn't want to leave the warm bed, so I wallowed in what I knew was her scent, distinct from the scents of her soap and hair oil. Her husband hadn't returned. None of the men who had gone for the night shift had returned. On both sides of the road, women waited sullenly for a vehicle from the construction company to come around the far bend, over the bridge on the Khahare stream.

I had already changed into my school uniform when Mother hurried home without any fodder for the buffalo. She threw her sickle and namlo into the hibiscus bush by the waterspout and came to the woman's shack. Mother started to cry when she saw the woman and led me away, put me in Father's room and locked me in. The air was curdled with foreboding. But I knew how to steal around the house. I pushed my head through the horizontal bars on the window, climbed out, walked the ledge to the balcony on Grandfather's side and climbed to the slate roof. If I could lie still, without dislodging a tile, nobody would know where I was.

But Mother saw me right away, even as a jeep careened around the corner near our orchard and stopped at the crossroads by the bus-stop. The owner of the teashop across the road from our house strode to the jeep, waving his hands to dismiss the women who wanted to flock around the jeep. The teashop owner was the only man around; the men in the jeep wouldn't talk to the women anyway. When the jeep sped off, leaving the teashop owner to emerge from the thick cloud of dust left in its wake, the women stirred as a single body and approached him. But Mother screamed at me. The woman stood by my mother until I started my climb down.

When I reached the road, skirting well away from women who might clip the side of my head for having climbed the roof, the shacks along the road had become something other than domiciles: they were the instrument for an eerie music made in equal parts of silences and screeches, of doors and window shutters flailed about the hinges, the zip and tear of a blouse being torn, the throaty, hoarse sobs of a woman suffocating against the chest of another, voices lost after the first puncturing scream, stupefaction, hysteria.

The tunnel under the mountains had collapsed. Dozens

of men working through the night had been buried. The construction company had dug everybody out before announcing who had been injured and who was dead.

The woman escaped Mother's clutch. Another woman, a wife whose husband had gone to work early that morning, tried to grab her and bring her back from the abyss of hysteria, but she wrenched herself free, hitched up her sarong around her knees and ran. She ran into the mustard fields that stretched unbroken to the big river. She parted the yellow sea and left nothing in her wake but sunlight undulating on mustard leaves: tricks played on the eyes, a woman with pale, soft limbs dissolving into the colours and light of the valley, dissolving whatever might have passed in the minutes, the hours, the night before.

Mother screamed after me, but I knew better. I ran around the mustard fields, jumping over fresh dung on the narrow stone-hedged path that went down to the river, jumping over low bamboo gates, racing through jetropha fences between properties. I knew I had to reach the woman before she reached the river.

I saw her reach the rocky bed of the Khahare stream. She stumbled, fell, got up and ran on. I must have called her name, because I must have known her name then, but I remember that she didn't turn back, she didn't hear me over the roar of the river, over the sound of all the other women along the road shout for those who had been pulled from the rubble, dead, dead, dead. I quieted the roar of my own heart in my ears, in my throat, and ran towards my woman. But she disappeared behind a clump of cacti.

Now I know I could have searched for her—tracked her along the river like an aboriginal hunter on the National Geographic Channel, or intuited her location. Or called to her, reasoned with her, held her, kissed her tears away, pleaded with her, hurt her into submission if I needed. But that morning, she disappeared from view, buried under the weight of what had passed. I listlessly searched the fields along the river, the large rocks with their secret caves. I couldn't return home because Mother waited, surely, with a fresh reed switch or a stalk of stinging nettle.

Death was not trivial in a village where natural death was a rare, celebrated affair, protracted sometimes for weeks as the old refused to make their journey to the world beyond. It was a sin to watch, sometimes, the dead being carried away, while it was a sin at other times to not touch someone who'd just died. But it was always necessary to participate, to join a procession or step out of its way as it followed the wail of a lone conch, winding its way down to the river where the dead were cremated. The homes of the bereaved attained a halo of grief, of being touched by the heavenly in a village preoccupied with the mundane. Everybody waited for the tenth or the thirteenth day to mark the end of mourning, a day when salt was welcomed again, shared by tongues hurrying to talk of something else than death.

After an hour of searching, I reached the river. Several pyres crowded the stretch of the riverbank marked for the dead. Some were already lit, burning black or bright, men tending the fire stepping back with smoke-stung eyes, using a length of green bamboo to poke at the logs, break the body into smaller chunks, limbs huddling around the head and the ribcage to burn quicker. Half of the village—women, children included—had gathered to watch. I weaved my way through the crowd, checking for uncles and aunts who might send me home. I steadily crept closer to the pyres, trying to see who was on which pyre by matching the people preparing or tending to the stacks of logs. The teashop owner who had received the news of the disaster in the morning was standing beside a pyre that seemed prepared, complete, yet unwilling to go, like a student with a full suitcase refusing to board the bus that would take him to a boarding school in the big city.

Like a hive of bees reacting to a smoking torch brought under it, the crowd shifted its collective focus to a figure that came running, screaming out of the bushes at the far end of the cremation grounds. My woman! Shirt torn down the front, a gash on her arm, sarong still hitched to the knees. She ran towards her husband's pyre. I elbowed my way through the crowd that had congealed at the front to get the best view of what would follow, and ran towards her. The teashop owner waited near the pyre like a goalkeeper waiting for the football to be shot in his direction. My woman tried to throw herself on the pyre, but the teashop owner grabbed her, plucked her off the ground and carried her away. I reached her just then. The teashop owner lifted his hand as if to backslap me, but when he saw me clinging to the woman, he didn't do anything.

'Babu!' The woman pointed to her husband, now on the pyre, shrouded except for the face, balls of cotton in his nostrils, one eye refusing to close entirely, the purple of a bruise depressed over one brow. I grabbed her arm and tugged her away from the pyre, away from the crowd.

She sobbed once, a cold sob that seemed to take air to the depths of her womb. The silent crowd had grown even quieter—even the crackle of the fire from the farthest pyre was louder than any sound that the crowd made. Her nails dug into my back as she looked at the world around her: the line of pyres, the sea of dumbstruck faces, and the teashop owner fretting quietly, arms outstretched to shoo us away, as if we were carrion birds alighting at a feast. She pushed herself up on one knee and I instinctively grabbed the torn halves of her shirt, worried that the world would see the pink bruises on her breasts. She unhitched her sarong to cover the punctures and rashes and welts on her legs.

She led the way and I followed. We walked away—not along the main road, for which we would have had to part the crowd—but along the river, along its gentle curve away and back so that once we walked around a cornfield, the crowd and the pyres disappeared beyond the cusp of the east. After half an hour, she sat on a low rock in the river and washed her feet. She cried a little, splashed water on her face and cleaned her hand.

Then she took my hand. We left the river behind, cut through Grandfather's fields, and skirted around the mustard fields near home. Mother was waiting in the yard, tired, surrounded by the wives of other men who lived in rooms rented from us. These were the fortunate, women whose husbands had returned, women who now had the nasty job of persuading the less fortunate into a life of widowhood. The woman led me to the waterspout, squeezed my hand and went to sit quietly in the circle of the women who waited for her. I sat under the waterspout, wearing the school uniform that I had run away in, as the women took away from the woman all signs of married life: the gold she wore on her ears, the red tika on her forehead. They tried to break the lone blue bangle on her wrist, but it was made of soft plastic, once upon a time an unbreakable promise. She took it off and handed it to the teashop owner's wife, who broke it between two stones.

Over the next month I tried to avoid the woman, although Mother sent me to sleep in the shack after the thirteen days of mourning were over. The woman had grown quiet, never once stirring in her sleep—I couldn't tell if she slept the sound sleep of the dead or if she never slept, never allowed herself to slip into the realm of dreams. She didn't cry much. Instead, she went to the company office with a sheaf of papers, spread them on the bed each evening to study which documents had been signed and stamped, which ones needed to visit the office the next day, what had been subtracted and what had been added. At the end of the month, she pressed some money into my hand after Mother refused to accept the rent she owed and left the village.

Until the next tenant moved in, I made the shack my refuge from the daylight outside, hiding from friends who called me out to play. The plank bed by the window was bare. I'd lay there, hands thrown behind my head, staring at the walls, at the ceilings. I am sure that I remember the woman's name in the dreams when she comes to me, throwing open the door of the shack and walking in with the bright daylight behind her. But I can't remember her face or her name anymore. Instead, she has left behind me with an odd affection for a host of names and eyes and mouths that plastered the ceilings and the walls of her home: Jina Tamang, Kimi Katkar, Jaya Prada, Rekha, Ranjit. Perhaps she remembers my name. Perhaps she still wakes with an ache by her side where my head used to nest on her shoulder as we read *Mayapuri* and laughed, embraced and shared a bed.

FORTUNE

The chill that had developed between them over the property along the highway to Gorkha had thawed by Dashain—Lok Nath listened to his younger brother Sashidhar's counsel and agreed to give Sudha's hand away in marriage to the boy Sashidhar had picked. Lok Nath's wife, Sayapatri, and daughter, Sudha, then went over to Sashidhar's home to help plaster the cracks in his walls and paint the facade with lime and ochre. It took the brothers a few more weeks before they could sit together in silence and wait for the butcher and Surya to arrive after dusk to pass around a hookah. One evening, Sashidhar asked Lok Nath if he would sell the bull buffalo in the cattle shed. The butcher said nothing, but he grinned and nodded, looking once in Lok Nath's direction, then in the direction of the buffalo.

Lok Nath walked to Abu Bazaar the next day. The bridge over the Chisapani stream was crowded with pilgrims and goats waiting for the morning bus to Gorkha. From a safe distance, he looked at Sashidhar's new house: a squat square of mud and stone perched atop a slope dropping towards the Marshyangdi, a few paddies between the house and the river. Yes, it was in the bazaar, and perhaps in a few years it would be worth something, but it looked poor. Their father had owned many more of such paddies and many more heads of cattle than Sashidhar and Lok Nath did. A dozen dependent families had worked their father's holdings. Lok Nath saw how petty the animosity with Sashidhar had been. He felt pity for his brother and the smallness of his greed.

A week later, Lok Nath and his companions tried to find a footing on the dung-slicked floor of his cattle shed. The bull buffalo pulled on its leash and resisted them, lashing with its tail to catch Surya on his face, kicking with its forelegs and lunging at the butcher and flooring him with its head, sending him sliding on the morning's dung. Even in the tumult of the animal being dragged away to slaughter, it showed proof of its virility, as if to beg Lok Nath to stay the murder.

The butcher picked himself up and slapped the buffalo's rump with affection. Lok Nath caught the animal's nose ring and brought it to its knees. Its companions in the shed stamped their hooves and pulled their ropes, raining the moult of musty old thatch on the men.

'Big one, this one.' The butcher tried to catch his breath. Surya washed his face in the next buffalo's full trough.

'Of course you will say that.' Lok Nath grinned. 'You are

getting the better of the bargain.' Moments before, the butcher's plump hand had extended thirty green notes exquisitely, expertly fanned. There had been regret in the butcher's eyes. 'You are getting a good bargain, but I am losing my bull buffalo.'

'Three thousand rupees, Lok Nath, and you are still grumbling about money. I know I am only a butcher, and a greedy one, but letting yourself stoop to my level! What will people say?'

They all laughed. Even as he noosed a weathered rope around the buffalo's horns, Lok Nath could feel the thick roll of money slide in his pocket.

'Why don't you send me one kilo of goat meat?' asked Lok Nath in jest.

Surya laughed. 'This uncle giving away goat meat for free? Won't the sun rise from the west before that happens?'

'Why disparage me with clichés every chance you get, Surya?' The butcher took the leash and tugged at the buffalo. 'You are well fed on my innards every day, still you disparage me in front of friends.'

'I am not disparaging, only calling you greedy. Truth is truth, no?'

'Just pull the buffalo,' said the butcher and blew under his nails.

They were coming straight for Lok Nath: his wife, Sayapatri, after heaving off a load of fodder, and Navaraj, Sayapatri's twenty-year-old nephew, grabbing the buffalo by the horns even as he greeted his elder brother Surya.

The butcher had once been a teacher at the high school and the young were still deferential to him. So he talked Navaraj down: Look at how much work it is for Sayapatri to keep the buffalo fed, he said. Look how badly Lok Nath needs cash, and look how much better off Sashidhar is, now that he sells milk and buffalo calves.

'Who likes to sell cattle they have raised and fed?' Navaraj asked. The butcher pretended not to hear, so Navaraj turned to Surya, who worked for the butcher now. The boys had come to live with their aunt Sayapatri after their father died, leaving them with a small patch of land and two dry paddies high on the mountains to the north. Surya scowled back, so Navaraj turned to Sayapatri.

But when Sayapatri went into the house without turning to look at the bull buffalo, Navaraj cut open the bundle of grass she had cut and stood there with his hands on his waist, watching Surya and the butcher lead the animal away.

Twenty-two hundred rupees were left by the evening, after buying mosquito nets and new utensils and putting up a deposit with Kanchha Sunar for the jewellery he would make for Sudha's wedding. Lok Nath forced Navaraj to pocket a hundred-rupee note. 'You are still young and I have rarely been able to provide for you,' Lok Nath said. 'It is your age to eat and drink and wear nice clothes. Your aunt and I are old, your sister is still too young to understand, but you are young, and you are like my own son.'

Navaraj stood there awkwardly, staring at the plumed portrait of the king on the green note, as if this affection was too sudden and strangely placed on a hundred-rupee note. At home in the evening, Lok Nath carefully prepared a hookah and waited for Sashidhar to show up. But Sashidhar didn't come. It was the butcher who came instead, with a newspaper and a flashlight.

'Look,' he said, 'they are going to build a dam here. A factory first, and now a dam.'

'They can build whatever they want. What difference does it make to us?'

The butcher laughed. 'It made all the difference when they built the Rubber Factory over in Deurali, didn't it? Your brother became a milkman, and I became a butcher. Who knows what we will become when the dam comes to our village? Maybe Navaraj will become a fisherman.'

'This place was nothing,' Lok Nath said. The valley had once been full of tigers and jackals and cattle-sheds. Then China built a road through it and pastures became real estate. Families from the mountain hamlet of Abu Khaireni descended to live in new clusters in what had been their pastures. New paddies were created, springs were re-directed. Within a decade, there was a school in place. Buffalo-eating Newar shopkeepers brought shrines of the Kumari and Bhimsen and started trade in textiles and hardware. New families arrived. Their lineages could not be verified but they had to be accepted because they presented credentials. Children played in the village lanes, but they all looked unfamiliar, and Lok Nath could no longer tell from their faces who their father or mother was. As long as the new arrivals didn't ask to eat at his hearth or ask for his daughter's hand in marriage, they were acceptable. They bought milk and vegetables from the old families, if not land to build their own homes.

The Rubber Factory had brought a lot more people than the highway—some engineers and officers of good castes, others labourers of inferior castes. Now there would be a dam, and it would bring engineers and officers from America, Japan, Germany, China, Korea, Canada, Britain. 'Multinational corporation,' the butcher said in his teacher's voice.

'They will bring new jobs.' Lok Nath saw swarms of heavy construction machinery on the highway.

'They'll bring chaos, that's what.' The butcher rolled up the newspaper and put it by the flashlight. 'The government has never seen construction of this scale in a populated space before. There are things to be duly considered. Any sensible person will see these things. Like, how much is a tree worth?'

'This is the modern age,' Lok Nath said. 'This is 1985. They are big people, educated people, intelligent people. If they can stop a river and force it into a tunnel, you think they can't duly consider things?'

'Intelligent people!' The butcher shielded the embers

with his palm and blew. 'Intelligence is the uncle of corruption. They know how to do this and that, but at the end, you and I are left with the peel, and they will not only take the fruit, but also cut the tree down. That is why! Intelligent people!'

'You have no trust,' Lok Nath told the butcher. 'If they cut one tree, you can plant another. Why grumble? I keep animals, you only kill them. There are plenty of trees in the forest if I need fodder. Does man make trees? No! Soil makes trees. Let one man cut one tree. Earth will make a hundred more trees.'

'You are backward, Lok Nath,' the butcher replied.

'You are forward, progressive, developmental, what not. That's why you are a butcher now. We made you the first headmaster of a school, now you sell meat to the men you taught.'

'We all become butchers, by and by. By and by, everything will be bought and sold.'

'You are a prophet now!'

'No.' The butcher stood abruptly and walked to the cattle shed. Lok Nath could hear him counting cattle. When the butcher returned, he grinned as he reached for the hookah.

But the butcher was right. Multinational corporations came to Khaireni. Lok Nath sat under his mango tree and listened to the new small talk. Somebody's son became a lorry driver for the Project and was caught, fist in jar, stealing from the site. The old families tore down their houses in the old village to build lines of hovels along the highway, rickety but of seasoned old timber, dark but with plenty of cracks for the sun to shaft through. Labourers trickled in at first, then their brothers, cousins, friends and villagers came. Bangladeshis, Indians, and Nepali men from all corners of the country came to crush stones and lay masonry and tunnel through the mountain.

Heavy machines with CATERPILLAR in ominous black typeface tore up the asphalt of the highway and settled a thick layer of dust on the crops and fruit trees. Vegetables from the kitchen garden became inedible, but vendors with vegetables trucked in from Yampa and Chitwan pushed rickshaw carts around the village. No longer was the river heard, but the incessant drone of heavy machinery grinding stones, moving loads of blasted rock. Thirty children died in accidents or disappeared within a year. Human excreta as public display arrived. The village of a few hundred people swelled to accommodate six thousand labourers and their families. Water had to be diverted for the burgeoning town. Families without natural springs within their fields lost their crops and sold their land to become shopkeepers, lost their money double quick, and left the village for other projects where nobody knew the names of their grandfathers.

A year passed without a bull buffalo in the village—the

butcher and his rivals bought up all the young male calves. Pandey's sickly bull buffalo replaced Lok Nath's in the village. The twenty-one hundred rupees Lok Nath received from the butcher had lasted three months—goat meat every week, new clothes for Sudha to keep up with her peers at school, bags of whitewash for the house, trips to the decrepit new cinema, samosas and vegetables and a pressure cooker that made Sudha laugh each time it startled Sayapatri in the kitchen. Money, which had once been useful only while travelling outside the village, now made the difference between cooking the evening's curry with a tomato in it, or without, which made all the difference to a tongue that had lately acquired new tastes packaged in the shiny foil bags in Newar Kanchha's shop.

Newar Kanchha's father had been a cattle-hand for Lok Nath's father, but Newar Kanchha seemed to have picked up his hereditary mercantile character. When families from Abu Khaireni village had moved down to the valley, Lok Nath had given Newar Kanchha and his wife a small plot of land at the end of the village, under a rocky outcrop overlooking the river. What had been uninhabitable to Lok Nath—a patch of dust filled with stones, no drinking water, and the hill rising immediately behind in mossy faces of stone—had become prime real estate because the highway touched it.

Lok Nath was returning home from an afternoon of walking through the town when he saw a swarm of children outside Newar Kanchha's house. 'Isn't this too much cement?' Lok Nath asked the wiry Newar Kanchha, whose deference towards his father's employers had morphed from sincere to ceremonial. Newar Kanchha did not answer immediately. Instead, he walked to an Indian labourer pouring cement into forms on the ground.

'Isn't my money,' he replied, ambling back to Lok Nath but keeping his eyes on the workers, pausing to shout insults. 'Germans want a clean ground. I said—there is dust on the ground, once the rains come it will be muddy. But they want clean, clean. They are buying me two fridges. Refrigerators like in shops in Pokhara. You have never seen? You can make ice in it, keep Coca-Cola and beer cold. Germans want one fridge just for beer, chilled beer. That's why.'

'So much cement,' Lok Nath said. 'What will you do when they finish building the dam and the Germans go away?'

'That will come when it will come. Now I want the Germans to come, drink chilled beer and pay for it.'

That they will, Lok Nath told Newar Kanchha as he walked into the shop. There were posters on the walls of beautiful European women holding bottles of beer. Colours exploded from the rough shelves: chocolates, instant noodles, cigarettes, toffees, biscuits, teas, cheeses, potato chips, soft drinks not yet in a refrigerator. Colours exploded on Newar Kanchha's wife in her shiny nylon sari and grim makeup, her head uncovered even after Lok Nath cleared his throat to dispel the possibility that, perhaps, she hadn't recognized him yet.

A girl asked for a packet of tart candied mangoes. Cement was mixed and poured, instructions given and complaints made. Children came and went with their double bubble gum or peppermint balls. Wage earners bought enough rice and lentils for the evening and the next day, and with the remaining money bought whatever cheap alcohol or chewing tobacco seemed affordable. The sharp chill of a river valley evening crept in with the steep shadows of the southern mountains. Lok Nath watched the highway and the infested, maggoty life that enveloped it and asked: When did this happen? Where was I? He finally called Newar Kanchha's wife and bought a packet of coconut biscuits, not because he was hungry or because he liked biscuits, but because, in that moment, he felt the urge to remember that he could buy with cash something he had no desire for.

Lok Nath gave the biscuits to Sudha, who made a face. 'Why do you spend money at Newar Kanchha's?' she asked.

'They smell like coconuts,' he explained to Sudha.

'I know,' she said as she took the biscuits. 'But, why do you give money to that Newar?' She pushed the biscuits under the thatch by the door. Sayapatri didn't allow packaged food in the kitchen—who knows what is in it, and who knows who made it, she'd say. Only after Sudha sulked away did Lok Nath remember that Sudha had quarrelled with Newar Kanchha's daughter over a hair-band which he had bought for Sudha but Newar Kanchha's daughter accused of stealing from her. Out of an old habit, he walked to the cattle shed to let the calving buffalo lick his hand.

Although Lok Nath realized that a bull buffalo would have been good insurance in times of emergency, he was glad that Sayapatri didn't have to labour for as much fodder. Milk was in plenty until the dry months came, as they inevitably do, and he was left with only one buffalo. He told his clients to ask Sashidhar for milk, and Sashidhar consented after Navaraj consented to help with the cattle. Soon, Sashidhar started talking about money. Lok Nath would sit with his hookah in the evenings and Sashidhar would come beaming, brimming with suggestions and questions. Why don't you sell this piece of land and buy that shop instead? Why don't you move by the highway, you can build a house and rent it out and live on the rent, never lift a fallen twig again. Lok Nath refused for long to sell his land, but life made little demands that couldn't be ignored any longer.

Some people still called Khaireni a village, but others had started calling it a town. Old names disappeared and new names were created—Kahare Khola became Milan Chowk after a bridge was built to connect Prithvi Highway to Gorkha and the stream below the bridge disappeared from sight. Chisapani became Bazaar. What had been glades and streams came to be named after a house or a person or another town. Names by which Lok Nath knew the locales were no longer in use. Sashidhar and Lok Nath stood outside the butcher's shop one afternoon lamenting the fact.

'Why are you complaining? Has one man covered the sun with his palm and blocked it out? Change is change. The only unchanging thing in universe.' The butcher hacked at a thick bone to get to the marrow.

'Old men have reason to complain,' Surya picked up the scrap and marrow and threw them into a boiling pot. 'In their youth they have seen one thing, and now things are different. It has to be difficult. Not everybody has philosophy like yours.'

'Now you are an old person?' snapped the butcher.

'Surya has a point,' said Sashidhar.

'Fat point he has.' The butcher whacked at flies with a blood-caked rag. 'Wheel keeps turning; potter makes good pots today, bad pots tomorrow, nothing is certain. But what is certain and unchanging? That his wheel keeps turning. Only constant in life is inconsistency. Better to learn.'

'My point exactly,' Surya turned the hose on the floor and the chopping block. 'Wheel keeps turning, but what does the pot know about that? Nothing. Why should old people in the village have to deal with trucks killing their grandchildren and men raping and selling their daughters to India? Three girls have returned from Bombay so far, and nobody knows how many more from this village have been sold there. Did these men know evil like that?'

'Why are you talking about Bombay?' asked Lok Nath. 'Talk about this village. That Bahun, with his English boarding school racket, is getting richer by the day.

Education is expensive, he says, and gives you one year of education for your children if you sign over half your land.'

'Daylight robbery,' Sashidhar muttered. Surya started convulsing with laughter. '*You* are saying daylight robbery, uncle?' he asked. The butcher also started laughing.

Sashidhar turned purple. 'People make rumours behind an honest man's back,' he said, which made Surya and the butcher laugh even harder.

'Sashidhar, at least aim big if you want to be cunning,' said the butcher. Lok Nath still didn't understand. Surya told the story between laughing fits. Sashidhar had caught the money bug quite superbly, it seemed: he had expanded his clientele from five teashops to some seventeen teashops and households, including a senior officer at the Project.

As his supply of milk diminished, clever Sashidhar decided that a few scoops of water from his pond would solve his supply-side problems. Months passed without a complaint. One morning, however, fortune took a turn. Sashidhar had just stepped out of a particularly garrulous woman's shop when she immediately followed him outside and brought the heavens down with her protests. People gathered. She had found a tadpole in the milk. Lok Nath laughed uncontrollably.

Sashidhar was quiet for the rest of the afternoon as they walked from this man's shop to that new place, marvelling at the new photocopy machine in the stationery store, watching boys and young men from old families sneak in and out of the only shop that sold buffalo-meat dumplings, wondering if there would be very many of the old families left in the town. Chinese engineers and labourers alike walked in their blue cotton overalls, each indistinguishable from any other, except for an occasional gold tooth which flashed with superiority. Three bicycle stands had opened for business; even middle-aged women were paying three rupees an hour to learn how to ride a bike.

'I think I will go,' Sashidhar said once they reached Chisapani. Lok Nath decided to while away the evening. He walked northwards again, reaching the Chinese Bridge at the end of the settlement, and walked back. People gathered around the temple that was yet to be built, although the ground had been broken the year before.

Right by the temple was Khurshid Kashmiri's bangle shop, a little foldaway wooden contraption. Lok Nath heard laughter in the shop as he passed it. Evening descended slowly. Lok Nath reached Chisapani and turned back again. Fluorescent lights lit up the shops. Adhikari's textile shop enchanted him with its thousands of bundles of cloth arranged by the colours, imperceptibly shifting from green to yellow, or green to blue, or green to brown and red. He paused outside Khurshid's shop when he heard the same laughter once more. Although it embarrassed him a little, he decided to look in.

Sayapatri sat on the floor while the Mussalman's wife tried to push a delicate blue bangle over her wrist. The women talked and laughed. Lok Nath felt himself choke. For a minute he felt exactly like the first time he had inhaled tobacco, a very long time ago. His eyes glazed and nausea knotted his guts. My wife's laugh, he thought, and I couldn't recognize it? He tried to recall the last time they had spoken about anything that was not a buffalo, or the need to marry off Sudha.

Why should I be blamed, he thought, why should I think I have failed? What does one talk to a wife about? But it didn't go away, the suddenness of that sour moment, the leaden weight of walking away from the sound that should have been most familiar to him.

That night, Lok Nath asked Sayapatri about her cough and her short breath. 'Are you sure nothing has gone worse?'

'Are you wishing my death already?' she asked.

'Talk auspicious, wife.' He found his voice unusually gentle towards her. He told her about the bangle shop. 'When did this happen, wife?' His voice trembled and caught. 'Where was I while this happened?'

Sayapatri turned to face him. He wondered how to touch her face with his calloused hands. There, beneath the wrinkles, he could still see the well of laughter he had been privy to as a young man. Her eyes had lost their brightness, her hair was thin and dull and her hands dry.

'For four years we haven't been to the hospital,' he said.

'If the gods are happy, we won't have to for another four years.'

'I think we should, wife. Tomorrow.'

'I am hale and hearty. Why are you excited to waste your money?'

'It is no waste to make sure,' he said. How many people had died of weak hearts and lungs in the past years?

'It is the roads that they don't repair,' Sayapatri said.

'It is this and it is that. Still, we should go to the hospital just to make sure.'

'Money doesn't grow on trees, unless you have found one.'

'I am saying this much with love. I fear for your well-being, and mine, and you keep telling me it is about the money. If we live another day, I will make another bundle of money for you, wife. But let's just go and see what the doctors have to say.'

'Whatever you say.' Sayapatri closed her eyes. 'I am not dying tomorrow or day after. Not before Sudha is married,' she said.

The Regional Hospital in Pokhara was not very crowded at all. Lok Nath wanted to get Sayapatri to have her eyes checked, while she insisted nothing was wrong with them. A few medical students found the old couple in the waiting room and checked their pulse, blood pressure, and the colour of their tongues. 'Look at the ceiling, breathe deep, cough,' they said.

They told Lok Nath that he had a heart murmur, which to him sounded unseasonably romantic, but apparently it was no laughing matter. 'Although it isn't exactly a crying matter either, uncle,' a large-eyed, curly-haired Brahmin girl told them. Doctors came and went, nurses rushed around as Sayapatri waited with her pupils dilated, unable to walk a step without holding on to Lok Nath's arm. 'Dandy old couple,' one young doctor called them as he hit Lok Nath's knee with a rubber hammer, which gave him strange sensations in his inner thigh, as if he were being touched. He enthusiastically collected all the small chits and forms and slips and recommendations and redirections handed to them by doctors, nurses and administrators. Khaireni was a distant memory; he wanted to play in the bright whitewashed hallways of the hospital. He left Sayapatri in the corner where she dozed off and found in his heart a voyeur who delighted in wondering how heavy that goitre must be, or how the man must have burned his arm.

Sayapatri was still disoriented when evening came, but she chided him nonetheless for not finding a bus ticket to return to Khaireni that evening. 'What is there to return to?' he asked frivolously. He knew his wife wouldn't take his remark as seriously as he had hoped to mean it. He took her to Mahendra Pul. People dropped tangerine peels to see how deep the gorge was, waiting for it to disappear cleanly, without touching the sides, which never happened. 'There should be a river like this everywhere,' Lok Nath said to Sayapatri, 'for people to get rid of their troubles.'

'They get rid of their troubles often enough here,' said a stranger. 'Two or three individuals throw themselves over the bridge every month, sometimes in broad daylight and in everybody's view. Some scream, some don't.' The stranger's remark sat foul in Lok Nath's ears. With her vertigo, Sayapatri refused to look down.

The next morning, Sayapatri stayed in bed at their room in Mountain View Super Accommodation Hotel and Lodge, while Lok Nath went to the hospital to collect X-rays and reports. There was nothing to worry about, except, of course, the heart murmur and the cataracts in Sayapatri's eyes. Don't eat too much fatty or spicy food, they told him, and wait for a free eye clinic to come to your village to treat the cataracts. He returned happy.

Sayapatri was still sleeping, which made him even happier. She hadn't slept past sunrise since the day he married her, excepting the eleven days of confinement after Sudha's birth. He crawled into bed with her, after which she refused to continue languishing in bed.

'I am not returning without visiting Bindyabasini's shrine,' Sayapatri said. She carefully unfolded a corner of her sari and took out three bundles of rupee notes and coins, and counting each she recalled who had given her the money and for what purpose. Lok Nath's mind was elsewhere. They reached the shrine early but that did them little good because they had to wait for the bus to fill up with returning pilgrims before they could return to the lodge. Lok Nath and Sayapatri asked the waiter if there was any food left since it was so late in the morning. The waiter laughed and asked what they wanted. Sayapatri ate in silence but Lok

Nath called the waiter and asked him all manners of questions. Later, walking along the thronged shores of Phewa Lake, she told him that he had surprised her by talking for so long with a total stranger. She wanted to return to Abu as soon as possible, but there were still a few results to wait for, something to do with a sample of this or that. And the reports had to be shown to a doctor the next day.

The next morning, Lok Nath sat in a doctor's office in the Regional Hospital. A dull sky outside leaned into the garishly lit cubicle; Lok Nath found the plastic chair uncomfortable and the doctor's distracted manner annoying. 'It is nothing, really nothing,' said the doctor, a meek voiced young man with bulging eyeballs behind thick glasses that shrank his eyes into untrustworthy darts. He kept fumbling with the stethoscope and paperweight, repeating the same platitude, until a nurse swished in and curtly deposited a folder on his desk, grunted in acknowledgment and exited, shutting the door behind her. 'Your wife, you should have brought her. Concerns her, after all. If she is still in town, she should visit once. Nothing really, routine, commonplace in women her age and, ahem, her demographic. Not too much to worry. You say you are from Abu Khaireni?'

Sayapatri's heart was getting weaker. Commonplace, really, what with the life she had had to live; wife, daughter-in-law, mother, cattle to care for, fields to harvest, saving the best food for husband and daughter and from this day to another passing undernourished. She was walking outside

Mountain View with the bag of clothes, ready to leave. Lok Nath went straight to the cashier and settled the bill, an involuntary gasp escaping him with the realization that he had just enough money left to buy the bus tickets back to Khaireni. Sayapatri pressed her face to the bus window for most of the ride home. She woke up Lok Nath to point out villages and mountains in the distance, asking him to point out the houses of girls from Khaireni who had been married off to various villages along the road. Between villages came stretches of wheat fields and mustard fields, fenced by hedges of cactus that were in bloom. Lok Nath had walked through these villages a long time before there were buses or a highway. He became disoriented by the frequency of these settlements, by the speed with which they zoomed past, every house looked like every other from the speeding vehicle, and every person a vulnerable, passing blur.

The bus came to a screeching halt just west of the dam under construction. A young man wearing a leather jacket and sporting a ponytail cut his lip open on the seat before him. He jumped up and swore at the bus driver, but one look outside and his anger dissipated. He hurried off the bus and walked towards the crowd in the middle of the road.

'This afternoon,' Lok Nath heard somebody yell. He told Sayapatri to stay in the bus.

The bus driver honked his horn and received angry screams in return. Someone threw a stone at the driver, which bounced off the windshield. The driver climbed out of the bus in resignation. 'What happened?' he asked an onlooker.

'A car killed Maila Baje.' Lok Nath tried to peer over the shoulders of the crowd, but the sweating backs and pointed elbows repelled him. A car, blue and small, had run Maila Baje over, killing him. 'Motherfucking laws!' someone muttered. If you injure, you pay hospital costs. If you kill, you pay a paltry compensation that will not buy three cows. Half an hour after stopping by the corpse splattered on the highway, Sayapatri climbed off the bus and started home without telling Lok Nath. He saw her in the distance and followed her home.

The butcher's shop was filled with outraged people the next day. Maila Baje was in everybody's conversations. 'Let one man be killed, they will come and kill more. Accident? That is called an accident? Let us say it was accident to hit an old man who was looking after forty animals, mind you. Let us say car driver couldn't control, or an animal became frightened and started a stampede. Let us say Maila Baje didn't hear the car and stepped in its way. That is accident. But to back up the car to kill a man? That is murder. Let this one go, next one will do the same.' The butcher wiped his hands and stepped out of his shop, letting Surya clean up after him.

'We should call for a strike.'

'What's a strike going to do? I don't have the money to eat if I don't work for a day.'

Lok Nath stepped away from the crowd of young men

from the village and men who had come as labourers, and
students at Sri Ram Shah School.

'Simple logic,' said the butcher. 'If you don't work a day,
you lose a day's wage. But if nobody works for a day, the
Project loses millions. In crackling clean American dollars.
Strike for one day, and they will listen.'

'Your simple logic is neither simple, nor logical,' Surya
called out from inside the shop.

'Why are you disparaging me in public, Surya?' The
butcher seemed annoyed.

'Not disparaging, only pointing out. Truth is obvious to
everyone, no? The man who drove the car was a simple
man, big man's chauffeur, wage-earning man like you and
I.'

Everyone laughed at this. Does the butcher pay you a
wage, they asked. 'No, listen,' Surya insisted, 'what good
for anybody if he be lynched by people like us?'

'Working with me you started thinking like a butcher, eh
Surya?'

'You will bring everything to a halt over an accident?
What will you do the next time? Let the law take its due
course.'

'Friends,' the butcher called out over the din, 'Surya is
calling it accident, I am refusing to call it accident. A matter
of principle.'

The matter of principle was translated into action the
next day. Nobody reported to work for the early morning
shift in the tunnel that was being built from the dam to the

power station situated some sixteen kilometres down the highway. Rocks went unblasted, rubble went uncleared, the tunnel went untunneled. The village went about its business—the butcher sold more meat than usual, children played with their fathers, spontaneous football games broke out in the alleys. Towards the evening, kites climbed and people cheered. The strike was a festive success even without much agitation accompanying it.

The butcher invited people to his shop at around eight in the evening and informed everyone about the progresses been made through the negotiations. The Project agreed to establish a fund to compensate victims of road accidents that occurred between the dam and the power station. There would be a new clinic that would treat accidental injuries and refer them to the Regional Hospital if needed. 'Simple negotiations, simple gains,' the butcher told his congregation. 'Important thing is to remember how it was achieved. Through persistence and demand for our rights. It is wrong to forgo one's rights.' People cheered.

The dry fields were sold for Sudha's marriage to a teacher from Chitwan. The groom's family originally came from Gorkha; they were of the old Kunwar stock and had made a sizable fortune after moving to the plains in the south. It was necessary to match hospitality with heritage. It was necessary to remember how things used to be. When

Navaraj wanted to marry a girl from Damauli, another piece of land had to be sold. Navaraj's new wife wanted to live by Bazaar, closer to the schools, closer to the medical dispensaries, closer to the vegetable vendors and milk-sellers.

May scorched the ground and raised it in billows behind large trucks plowing through the village. June came and settled monsoon clouds over the mountains' brows. The first threats of rain electrified the afternoons and stifled the earth and sweated the plants; periodically a storm whipped up the hills to bury the sky. Lok Nath paused under a power pylon and listened to electricity hum and crackle. How much of his father's lands did he and Sashidhar still possess? He could no longer remember how much land or where in the valley Sashidhar had bought or sold, but his own possessions had more than halved.

Most of the good paddies with their own cold springs were gone—either possessed by the Project, or sold for this or that expense. There had been a time when he could tell from which of his fields the morning's rice had come. There was no meaning to eating anymore; no relation between a man and his rice.

The Project completed its primary construction: the dam, the tunnel and the powerhouse would be ready for operation within a year. It was 1989; a wave ran through the world and a wave ran through Nepal. The butcher killed three goats and two buffalos in the greatest show of generosity Khaireni had seen in years. Sons, forgotten and often taken for dead, returned with garlands around their necks, striving to set themselves up as the next crop of selfless leaders. In the following months, the butcher had the most success; Lok Nath was invited to sit next to the butcher as the latter announced his intent to stand in the upcoming local elections as an independent candidate. Election mayhem ensued. Bribes became public.

Fathers expelled sons over ideological differences until a change in seasons necessitated their labour in the fields or the shops and rifts had to be mended. Flyers plastered the village with genial, servile faces and rousing slogans. Cultural troupes were engaged. Speeches were made. Free lunches of rice and goat meat was offered to anyone who professed to have voted for this candidate, and many ate twice, thrice, gleefully presenting their purple-stained thumbs as proof. The butcher was elected chairperson of the village development committee. He immediately declared the village a town, and himself the mayor. The villagers would have to pay tax beginning the following year, but there would be more of drinking water and school teachers. Surya became the manager of three butcher shops. A new law made it difficult for new butcher shops to open. Existing butcher shops became strictly regulated.

Sayapatri's illness came suddenly—or so it seemed to Lok Nath in perspective. It started with a cold, common enough, when a mid-July shower caught her between errands. She took ill harder than Lok Nath remembered of their life together. The fever lasted four days and Lok Nath took her pulse every morning and night. Becoming old, wife, he told her fondly. He asked Navaraj to send his wife to take care of Sayapatri that evening. She came and stayed the night. She cleaned out the mess Lok Nath had left in the kitchen, plastered the threshold in starlight the next morning, washed Sayapatri's clothes and cooked the morning meal. Lok Nath took Sayapatri's pulse and measured her temperature. The fever had subsided.

She continued to wheeze in her sleep. If Lok Nath pressed his ear to her back he could hear the disease in her lungs. 'I am strong,' she would tell him during the day, and she would be strong, too, but her lungs said different.

'If you could hear your breathing, wife—' Lok Nath began pestering Sayapatri.

'If you had work to do, you wouldn't sit and listen to my chest,' she said. 'Everybody becomes short of breath as they get older. What new thing are you telling me?'

'If I still had my musket I'd kill pheasants for you,' Lok Nath said. 'Hedgehogs are good, too. Quail and wild hen. Meat from hunts fortifies blood, gives strength.'

Lok Nath brought meat from Surya's shop every day and started cooking for Sayapatri. He liked to talk big in the kitchen, telling Sayapatri hunting stories which he had never told her before. He talked about an afternoon before their marriage, when he was hunting near her village, where he saw Sayapatri.

'That's when I saw you first, that afternoon.'

'I don't remember.'

'I remember,' he bragged.

'Did you think I would become your wife?'

'No. I was looking for quail.'

'Will you take me back?' she asked. 'Will you walk me back to my father's house?'

'Through that langur-infested forest? What is left there, wife, for you to go to? They have all died. No need for you to go.'

He wasn't half the cook Sayapatri was, but they fondly pretended otherwise. It proved futile, this gesture by Lok Nath, when he infected his own lungs from coughing too much in the smoke and soot of the stove. Sayapatri took over the kitchen duties once more, cooking outside where she had once cooked for the cattle.

Sayapatri's health was unsteady. She would recover for a few weeks, find the strength to run an errand that Lok Nath forbade of her, and the strain would make her ill again. She walked to Chhaku, where her brother's house lay in ruins, the home and hill of her birth and girlhood. The rain caught her on the way back; she had to walk back from the river because the dam had opened its floodgates, unleashing the river in its fullest over the dry expanse of rocks that she had crossed in the morning. She spent three hours under a tree, wet and feverish. She became very ill and had to be taken to Pokhara.

On a Saturday afternoon, two weeks after they left

Khaireni, Sayapatri sat up on the bed and ate more rice than she had eaten in four days. 'Bring me meat, husband,' she whispered.

'Dhat!' Lok Nath scolded. 'Doctors have given you medicines. You must watch what you eat, or medicines won't work.'

'I am cured,' she insisted. 'Look at this dal—you call this dal? My mouth is getting greedy, husband—my heart wants meat.' Lok Nath pretended to be worried and pretended to scold her, but he went to a bhojanalaya and asked a boy there to smuggle in a tiffin-box of chicken and broth. Lok Nath watched Sayapatri eat. This is no sick woman, he told himself, look how she eats! She asked him if he had also eaten meat with his rice. When he said no, she scolded him. 'You make me feel like I have sinned,' she said.

Lok Nath walked past the hotel where he had stayed with Sayapatri. The crudely painted signboard outside the hotel, the blue on the wall of its restaurant, the brief glimmer of recognition in the eyes of the boy washing cups behind the counter—they reminded him of himself watching Sayapatri sleep in the bed upstairs. He remembered the lightness in his steps during that brief holiday in Pokhara. He felt strong so he walked all the way to the shores of Phewa and ate a slice of pineapple from a cart under a peepul tree. Long after the sweetness of the fruit had vanished from his mouth, its fragrance lingered and reminded him of other things and moments of beauty that had passed. It rained a little as he walked back, so he waited inside a warm teashop, determined not to let the damp get to him.

Sayapatri died inside of a month from that afternoon.

After Sayapatri's death, there was very little left in the world. Lok Nath smoked his hookah and drank water to suppress his hunger if the effort to cook for himself tired him. He had never cooked just for himself, and no matter how often he tried, the effort felt scored with unhappiness. Sometimes he would rouse himself to prepare something Sayapatri had been fond of, and he would spend the entire day gathering beans or young bitter wild ferns, but by the time he finished cooking, he would recount too many things, too many moments: before that feast for the mind, his creation paled and appetite died. Navaraj's wife came to clean the house and cook every third day; Surya would send a cut of meat with her. On an impulse Lok Nath sold some land and donated part of the money to the Krishna temple that was to be built by a committee, ad hoc, led by the mayor, who assured him that one of the mirrors outside the temple would be dedicated in Sayapatri's name, her name etched on the glass.

Sudha returned for Sayapatri's annual. Being a wife hasn't been easy for you, Lok Nath asked her. Her husband was rarely at home and the in-laws were feeble with age. Sudha had gone from pampered daughter to dutiful daughter-in-law, and life had wilted her. Navaraj and his wife came with their infant son, making Sudha happy, but Lok Nath suspected there was more to the cheerfulness she showed around the newborn. She smiled and sang to the baby, but her eyes sang different. That evening Lok Nath stood under the jackfruit trees and listened to the guests huddled around Sudha and a fire, wiping each other's faces as they recalled Sayapatri's kindness and humour. Birds came to nest above his head. Vehicles raced on the highway and cicadas sawed themselves in the grass. Lok Nath stood. Waxy thick dark leaves of the jackfruit tree hid nested birds; their shadows cloaked him and settled above his eyelids and in the corners of his mouth, pushing his throat up and down as he stood with his hands behind his back, his back to the house where Sayapatri had lived. He cried for Sayapatri. Like an embrace, the subdued gurgle of a once mighty river raced up the mountainsides and rained upon the valley. The Rubber Factory helicopter climbed upwards into the dusk.

No new house had been built near Lok Nath's, but the bazaar where Sashidhar lived had grown busy, sprawling first like a runaway fire, then creeping skywards; ungainly boxes raised on stilts or stacked tall. The brothers still saw each other nearly every day—either Lok Nath walking the two kilometres to the bazaar to watch television, or Sashidhar walking with the mayor to Lok Nath's with cut betel nuts and cloves. Sashidhar had added three houses of three storeys each to be rented out to sixteen, seventeen, families, while he lived in a small house on stilts. He still had most of his land, and bought a small plot here and a paddy there whenever he had a substantial saving, which was often. Lok Nath enjoyed visiting Sashidhar at his new house, but the differences between their homes steadily grew. There were too many unfamiliar things—fridge, kerosene stove, heaters, television. Sashidhar liked drinking cold water now, wouldn't throw away the morning's leftovers, or give it away to someone who'd eat it, which disgusted Lok Nath. The land still gives, animals still multiply, there are hungrier people who would gladly eat in the evening what is cooked in the morning, Lok Nath thought.

The government started another Project in another part of the country. They had rushed in, but now they ambled their exit: some labourers had married local girls; some girls had grown into young women while the project lasted. As the exodus prompted, shanties and shacks were dismantled if salvageable timber made the effort worthwhile.

Cement and concrete emerged out of the pattern: whereas everything else—down to the bricks—could be chipped and carried away, concrete poured on the earth remained immobile, undecaying; an eyesore. The cement floor of Newar Kanchha's Famous German Beer Garden was left to testify for the erstwhile glory of loud red-nosed Bavarians drinking crates after crates of chilled beer as the natives watched with curiosity. The auto-mechanics plant where heavy machinery for the Project was serviced was now an open field of three-foot deep concrete with grease-filled, asbestos-lined trenches. Children tried playing football there, men tried playing volleyball, but concrete doesn't forgive falls. One last procession of bulldozers, cranes, concrete-mixers and trucks tore open the highway as they migrated to the next Project. Eerie quiet and a last blanket of fine dust settled on the emptying town. Shops became poorer and spectacles lost colour.

Pieces of land that had been acquired by the government for the Project could be taken back, or left with the government, in which case the original owners were compensated. Lok Nath came into money, heeded the mayor's advice and started eating in a teashop in the bazaar, two square meals a day and no worry for months to come. Sashidhar grumbled for a few days—'Live with me. If I fall sick, you can give me warm water. If you fall sick, I can give you warm water,' he said.

'If I die, Kanchha, I die under my own roof,' Lok Nath said.

'Go, die there then. And haunt the jackfruit tree. Even with your death you'll trouble everybody, make us carry you two kilometres more than if you'd quietly die here.' Lok Nath smiled at the thought of Sashidhar carrying him to the pyre.

Navaraj sometimes walked Lok Nath back to the old house where they had lived, where they had been fed and cared for by Sayapatri, where they had pampered Sudha. 'Don't come,' Lok Nath would tell Navaraj. 'Young bride at home. Shouldn't stray from home so late at night.'

'Look,' Navaraj would show Lok Nath the glowing dials on his watch, 'seven o'clock. I will be back in twenty minutes after taking you home.'

'Twenty minutes it takes me to walk home,' Lok Nath would say, and start walking away from the bazaar. But today he had insisted that Navaraj turn back. He wanted to walk alone, he said. He stopped at Surya's new supply shop. Surya and the mayor were making three other men laugh. The mayor looked much more youthful than Lok Nath—must be all the laughing and all the meat he gets, Lok Nath thought. The other men laughed no matter what Surya or the mayor said. Lok Nath felt pride in Surya, sitting behind the counter, a large calculator to his right, leather jacket draped over the back of the chair. The mayor saw Lok Nath.

'Why are you standing in the dark like a ghost?' the mayor shouted.

'Have you eaten, buwa?' Surya asked. When Lok Nath said yes, Surya grumbled that Lok Nath hadn't eaten at Surya's. 'Two sons you have in bazaar, but you eat at a teashop,' he said.

'It'd be trouble for your wives,' Lok Nath said.

'Nonsense you say, Lok Nath. When you die these boys will carry you to the ghat,' the mayor said. It irritated Lok Nath, this talk of his death. Sashidhar, Surya, the mayor—everybody reminding him how they would carry him when he is dead. He didn't say anything to the mayor or Surya, and when they slipped back into the conversation he had interrupted, they started laughing raucously again. Nobody called after him when he quietly slipped away in the night.

The road curved after the petrol pump and became a dyke raised over paddies. Jackals howled there, and ghouls lurked under the culvert bridge near the chautara at Thumki. Trucks approaching from the west blinded Lok Nath with their bright, broad headlights. Trucks approaching from behind scared him because he couldn't fully trust them to not run him over. He was getting tired of being scared of everything on the road when he twisted his foot and slowly fell to the ground.

He looked around in the dark to see if anybody had seen him fall, but he saw nobody else on the road. He didn't mind sitting there, planted in the fine dust by the roadside, but jeeps and buses and cars still went by, slowing down just a fraction before speeding past. Do they think I am a drunk, he asked himself. He tried to stand. He had twisted his right ankle very hard. When he took the first step forward he couldn't stop the tears of pain that streamed down his face and hung from the chin. But once he pushed himself past the pain, he managed to hobble to the chautara.

How late was it? Eight? Half-past? Lok Nath waited. After what seemed like an hour, three boys with torch-lights came from the bazaar.

'Babu!' Lok Nath called. The smallest of them started to run, but another boy grabbed his arm and cuffed his head. 'Why are running?' he scolded his friend. 'It is just an old father sitting on the chautara.'

Lok Nath shielded his eyes from the glare of three torchlights directed at his face. 'Come here, Babu,' Lok Nath called. The boys came closer. 'Do you know me?' Lok Nath asked.

'Aren't you Surya-dai's father?' a boy asked. Lok Nath still couldn't see their faces. He wasn't sure he had ever seen them before. If they were the sons of his cousins, they would have greeted him by calling him father or uncle.

'I am not his father,' Lok Nath said. He hadn't expected how much it would hurt him to say that, how much it would make him wish Sayapatri were here to hold his hands, or even how much he longed for Navaraj to carry him home. 'He is my wife's nephew,' Lok Nath said.

'Why are you crying?' the smallest of the boys asked. Lok Nath looked at his right ankle, which had swollen.

'His leg is broken,' the smallest boy whispered to his friends.

'Whose son are you, Babu?' Lok Nath asked him.

'Manohar Bagaley's,' the boy replied.

Lok Nath blinked a few times. There was no Manohar among the couple of old Bagaley houses. 'Whose grandson are you, Babu?' Lok Nath asked.

The boy fidgeted. 'I don't know my grandfather's name,' he said.

'What did others call him?'

'I don't know. He died very long ago.'

'Do you know where my house is?' The boys shook their head in the dark. Beams from their torchlights darted from his face to his foot, from the chautara to the road, into the gaping curtain of darkness behind Lok Nath, over the paddies, into the skies.

'We can tell Surya dai to come,' one of the boys spoke from the dark. 'I'll go with you,' the smallest boy pleaded. 'And I stay here alone?' the third boy asked, scared. Nobody was brave enough to return to bazaar alone, and nobody was brave enough to sit at the chautara with Lok Nath to wait for Surya.

'Go, three of you, go—bring Navaraj or bring Surya. Tell them I fell. Tell them I can't stand. Tell them I am alone and I can't walk.'

The boys ran off, waiting until they had crossed the culvert to start howling like jackals. A jackal answered from the edge of the forest: it ran closer, its howls came closer. Lok Nath saw lights in houses in the distance—lined along ridge across the valley, scattered like a constellation across the face of a hill. Those are young boys, he thought—they'll reach the bazaar soon and send somebody. When they hear that I fell and can't walk, they too will hurry. They will bring bigger torchlights and point them at the chautara as soon as they come around the bend on the road. They'll see me long before I see them—I'll only see the beams of light with which they will search for me, with which they will try to find me.

The light caress of a breeze made the peepul leaves rustle. Lok Nath closed his eyes and tried to think of all the other peepul trees he knew. He thought back to a time where, on any given day, he remembered the farthest distance he had walked from his home and the newest spring from which he had drank. He thought of the spread of the land he knew, and with one swat of the mind's capricious arm erased all the new houses, new roads and electricity poles, new temples and shops. And he started afresh, gingerly putting in their places the old hovels and houses he had eaten at, the paths he had walked, the trees he had climbed. He counted his father's fields where Sayapatri had worked. He counted the mango and wood-apple trees under which she would have sat at noon to fan her face and drink water before returning to back-breaking labour. He thought of the house in Khatrigaun where Sudha had been kept in confinement when she started menstruating. He thought of his father's house, long since sold to a new Newar family, where he and Sashidhar had sat in mourning after giving the funereal fire to their father's pyre. With pain in his right foot and with closed eyes, Lok Nath remembered as he waited to be found.

THE MESSIAH

Mother died and left me alone, wearing white, my head shorn, worrying about nothing, and with only two cowries to my name. Nothing tethered me to the village of my birth, so I sold what little I had and packed my bags. I found a place in Balaju, two minutes from the bus stop, fifteen minutes' walk from the vegetable market, the woody hills of Nagarjun five minutes away, three small cinemas in the neighbourhood, and plenty of immigrant parents who needed young college students to tutor their children. The landlords were a kind and clean Brahmin family from Lamjung who recognized in my features the age-old call for charity and kindness: the bachelor Brahmin orphan. The mother saw my head and white clothes and, taking pity on me, said, 'Mishra, for only a hundred rupees more, you can eat with us. What will a poor child like you cook? We are four in the family. One more plate of dal and greens for a child like you won't hurt my arms.'

Then, the Revolution of 1990 happened. The Congressi

boys and the Communist boys made fierce speeches in the
college. Four-stars and the hammer-sickle painted the walls.
Some said that the armed revolution against the king's
forces should be strengthened. Fools! What did they know
what an armed struggle is like? They flaunted the words
only because they knew none else; but now, two decades
since, they are reaping the harvest of throwing words around
too freely. And what good has this armed revolution done
for anyone? So many red flags, so much shouting and
chanting, so much accusing each other of betraying the
nation, of raping the Celestial Mother herself—and we
were all young boys, recently turned into men, easily broiled,
easier pushed. I thought of Nepal as a woman with the
ripest breasts, and the thirst in the hoarse throats of the
sloganeers would be quenched only with that motherly
nourishment of freedom from the oppressive aristocracy. I
thought, There is Mother again, and I get to be a son, not
just an orphaned child, but a son to all mothers.

But I have to say I was more afraid than most of my
friends. I wanted to amount to something, albeit without
shouting at anyone's face, without setting fire to stray dogs
that dragged through the streets, without carrying banners
blazing with obscene slogans. I kept to the rear. I thought,
The policemen are just as much Nepal's sons as I am, why
hurl stones at them? I did not agree or disagree with anyone,
but kept mostly to myself. I knew nothing of Mao or of
Koirala. I certainly did not know of the Iron Curtain or the
Cold War; I cared little that the wall had fallen in Berlin.

But it all came in thundering waves of information and a sense of injustice—listening to the BBC broadcast about demonstrations in Kathmandu, seeing doctors and teachers and lawyers take beatings for the cause of democracy, reading of the Jews in World War II Germany, then reading of Mandela's freedom. There was a sense of euphoria back then—we thought our Mother was in shackles, we'd free her and she'd walk free. We talked about the soil and pride and blood and the sunshine of progress and democracy. I mostly listened, never really said anything, because everything still seemed somewhat dramatic, somewhat play-acted.

Then, one day, I saw Haribansa Acharya and Madankrishna Shrestha with black gags over their mouths, kneeling in the middle of a cordoned crossroad. My friends brought cassette tapes of their performances, explaining how this was a satire on the royalist rulers, how that was a satire on the aristocratic smugglers of antiques and narcotics, how the third song was a parody about the state of untouchables and women in Nepal. I thought, Those men are of the people, giving us the most evanescent comfort of laughs, touching every ethnicity, every age, with their skits and parodies, the most any man did for this country. I felt they had emasculated me by beating me to the streets. But I was still afraid, and my landlords were afraid of what was to come. The police had started killing in the streets. Rumours of disappearances made us angry, but fear was still stronger.

⁓

It finally happened on glossy foreign paper, my move away from fear and into the arms of the writhing revolution. I was in college when boys sitting on the roof started kicking down low walls and pelting the police below with bricks. I had heard of the police hurling college students from the roofs of Amrit Science College. I had also heard of stranded policemen being beaten to death by farmer women in a village to the south of the city; Kirtipur, I think, but I don't remember. Suddenly the prospect of violence and bloodshed seemed real; destruction so proximate that the fear became an eerie elation. As if the prospect of death tempted us even more. Mother was in chains but we were free, and what was one life compared to the fate of the nation?

The police charged in, finally. We ran into classrooms, locking the police out. Some ran through the maze of hallways and stairs, dodging one blow of a thick bamboo stick here, another heavy boot there, pelting a policeman and fleeing to safety. I was punched in my ribs once, but someone pulled me into a classroom. We stayed locked in and laughed and chanted slogans, calling names at the king and the queen. After a while, the police left the college with two truckloads of arrestees. We came out and bragged about the injuries we'd received and made plans for the next day. There were many injured, but in that rush I paid no attention to the smaller gossip of what had transpired.

And so things went for a few days. I thought, There is one revolution in every lifetime, and this is mine. They killed people all over the country, numerous dissidents disappeared. Those who had been hiding in India returned heroes. People talked about all the Congressis and the Communists in jail. I took to pelting the policemen from a safe distance. A week later, someone brought a foreign magazine with a report on our revolution.

Four-stars and hammer-sickles galore! Flags, so many and so expansive you'd imagine that the entire Jyoti Textile Mills had become revolutionary, so tall that they seemed to reach the sky itself. It was a brilliant photo essay. Flags and raised fists, policemen charging with their cane shields and bamboo sticks, the king's palace in the grey background while the entire promenade before it was littered with the abandoned shoes of fleeing revolutionaries. Then there was a picture from my college—a sudden, brutal image on glossy paper printed on the other side of the world: a stumbling, tumbling figure. It shocked me. I could see the face of the falling man etched with the horror of certainty and behind him the faces of the men who had pushed him off the roof, angry but equally horrified. I used to know the man who fell. Perfectly good fellow, but there he was, suspended mid-air in a foreigner's picture, ogled at by people in don't-know-what corners of the world, a frozen relic of a historic moment, already distant and idealized.

I went home and worried, although I couldn't quite place where the worry stemmed from. It was a ghostly collage—that of him falling, bracketed by numerous other pictures where four-star and hammer-sickle flags waved brave over a deluge of arms and screams and scrambling feet.

I realized that his unmoving position in the charts of history was a bugle chiding me to rise and march, rise and march. I finally saw my impotency, my irrelevance. The world was changing around me, without my part in the big game.

Sometime in that long night, my tired mind welcomed sleep. I dreamed of an abyss; I was pasted against the bluest mountain face. A deep dark lip of nothingness with a sliver of a stream ran through the depth of the fall below me. A sky melted into the sheer trees above me, stretching endless across this dream and others. For some reason, I would not fall. Then I saw him hovering before me, the air barely moving his hair, a four-star badge pinned to the collar, thin trickle of blood spraying into the air in a crown of crimson beads arranged around his head. I tried to turn away to face solid earth—anything but the void, anything but the vertigo. Have you ever been trapped in such a dream? No matter how hard I tried to turn, the world turned with me, as if the firmaments were transfixed through my private horrors.

I could see the entire world without opening my eyes; his falling body now with the sheen of the glossy newspaper where he was assembled in a million tiny, flashing specks of colour, and a crisp shower of stars—falling in fours, falling with hammer-sickle zeal. The abyss only grew in its emptiness, because, instead of filling the space, the shower of stars only illuminated the vastness of the fall. My hair was dripping with sweat and I shivered with cold when I finally woke up.

I wish I'd thought of the nightmare as just another nightmare. After all, the nights were hot and terror abounded—it was no surprise that fear had seeped into my dreams. And who wasn't affected by that picture? If you looked at that falling martyr, something inside you would have said—It should have been you. Upon each of us was the taint that we hadn't taken the fall to arise celestially; waterworks and school gates, obscure crossroads and schools to be named after us martyrs. We—dirty-necked students with muddy toes and sacred cow dung in the kitchen, with millet-liquor on the breath of our fathers, with countless generations of untouchables among our mothers—we were awake, and we itched to mark Kathmandu as a part of our destiny. Not just for the xenophobic Newars and the cloistered, inbred aristocratic horde, but for every Nepali of every creed. We had real reasons to think we were strong, united by a cause. Those who are made to fall and wallow in submission, don't they eventually always rise to triumph? Isn't there at least one salvation due to each of us? No one should suspect the truth in that or what is there worth living for? Such was my awakening. I thought, How clearly I understand now! How clearly I see! This clarity is no illusion, and the call is as real as my time in this world. As real as the warmth of my bed, the sweat in my mouth, the smell of kerosene in the landlady's kitchen. As real as my dead mother's heartache.

That afternoon, I became one among the thousand tongues of a writhing serpent, the very Sheshnaag of the myths, eager to dictate the story of what would come next, for all of us, for the entire race. We were too many facing too many; blood boiled easily in that frenzy. It was a day filled with the usual sweaty jousting; sticks and stones and bricks, abandoned shoes and bottles filled with kerosene sweeping the road, the police with their usual surging bravado, few of them exaggeratedly vicious and others landing their batons lightly. Sweat and grime entered eyes and mouth, sand settled on tongue and teeth, feet blistered and hands ached. The sun got into the head and everything buzzed, an afternoon moment stretched like eternity and anything seemed achievable.

There was a Mainali from Dhankuta—a thorough revolutionary, very lively, very loud when he talked about the imminent change, straightforward and impossible to disagree with. He was wiry, short and Lenin-goateed, very hoarse after three days of screaming at the police, but cheerful nevertheless, his face shifting from a we'll-still-get-these-bastards grin to his comrades to a dark and furious come-and-get-this-you-monarchist-swine! in a single twitch. Then there was Rajesh, a Newar from Libang. What has become of his village now! Didn't he become a martyr in the latest Red Revolution? Was there anybody left in his family to accept the government purse for his slaughter at the hands of the army? I wonder if anyone ever got around to naming anything after Rajesh. Such were the boys, barely across the threshold of manhood, who thought it noble to die, who thought they'd be mourned.

You know the story of that afternoon. I remember looking back at where I had been, seeing smoking barrels in the distant crowd, drops of my blood trampled over by my rescuers as they jolted me from helpful hands to helpful hands and raced me to Bir Hospital.

Then I saw him—thin as a twig, all teeth and white of the eye when he grinned, staring at me. I was receiving his blood. When I lost consciousness again, I dreamed he was infested with tapeworms. He was scrawny, undernourished and pale after draining his blood to parasites. He was gone when I woke up but in that brief, jaundiced window of consciousness, I became nauseated by the conviction that I had been filled with tapeworm eggs. That terrible fragility of his frame—his glistening collarbone arching out from a deep hollow, a pair of floating, spectral eyes, that constant drone of placating words—apart from feeling a deep sense of remorse at having survived, my waking deliria and nightmares were filled with the tapeworm man, and there were sudden, restless bouts of sweaty, hard-breathing sleep.

The revolution was brief, just as its fruits were. Three weeks of agitation, a year of celebration, and prompt descent into corruption: this is the template that has been repeated, again, and again. There was talk of compensations for the dead and the injured, of felicitations and dedication of streets and crossroads. I couldn't bear the thought of being named in the same breath as those who had died, those who were being cynically dubbed 'living martyrs' for the crippling injuries that still keep them abed, unable even to voice their anger. When I saw my landlady weep for me after I returned to Balaju, I knew I had wronged her. I knew I had wronged my dead mother.

I fled Kathmandu, decided I would become a teacher in Gairigaun for a year or so, no matter what the revolution brought. I was resigned to my fate, so to speak. But, in those years, I also thought friendliness with fate brought a twisted freedom. Fate doesn't have to entertain a notion of fairness. What fool will expect any different? If on the sixth day the hand of Fate has written on our foreheads the course of everything that is to come, there will be no blame to give, no thanks to offer.

I sat in a bus at Thankot, in a dusk of night buses roaring downhill and juggernauts trudging uphill, with a picture of him in my shirt pocket. I had been recuperating from my grazing wound to the hipbone, eating the fruits and herbal tonics my fellow revolutionaries brought, when he surprised me. The tapeworm man was right there, between the fruits and the food. His eyes were languid even through the same big smile that I had seen. He had faded quickly—the paper was only five days old. His condolence photo had appeared late in the papers because there had been a scuffle over which political party had the right to claim him as their own. An all-party round-table had reached a consensus: they'd call him a people's martyr, raising him above inter-party politics. They had called it 'untimely'. He had given blood to me and returned to the crowded streets. He was shot twice in the chest. They didn't search for a blood donor for him because he was dead even before they grabbed him in the air. He was thin enough that the policeman's shotgun tossed him like a fistful of water. And the reporter had the audacity to describe the fall of my saviour, to use such a dainty metaphor for so violent a death! I looked at the picture again, but it was dusk outside and you know how newspaper photos are dotted. When I couldn't see his picture, the lines on his face became even more crisp, his eyes wider, that smile larger and terrifying. His radiance pressed into me, hovering *this* close to my face. He invaded my dreams.

Bhuvan Tripathi was his name, with the nom de guerre 'Biplav' within quotes, even in the obituary. His mother wrote to me through the village secretary when I sent a letter to her, thanking her for Bhuvan. I strained to find among the baroque phrases and salutations of the secretary the earthy, motherly words of Bhuvan's mother. 'Your blood runs in my veins too, mother,' I had written. 'Your son gave this orphan his life back.' Bhuvan's mother wrote back, talking at length about her dead husband, why Bhuvan was dark-skinned, how she lost him.

Bhuvan's father had migrated into the hills to sell bundles of Calcutta cotton cloth, married a poor Brahmin's daughter and settled in his father-in-law's village in Okhaldhunga after promising to never take his bride to his desh, to the heat and disease of his village somewhere south of the city of Ranchi. Bhuvan had grown up the dark and awkward child among his sturdier friends, teased for his father's bundles and his grandfather's penury. Bhuvan's mother had suffered for her husband's foreignness, too, her name forgotten, answering to Kali Sahuni after the colour of her husband's skin. I was afraid that she would accuse me in some way for the lifetime of hardship she'd had to endure— had her son not weakened himself by giving me his blood? Was I not the final punctuation to her story of injustice? That sun and the shouting of a broiling revolution, that need to scurry out of the oppressor's reach, the agility required not to get shot through the chest, the presence of mind demanded by mists of tear gas that set one hacking and crying—how could that scrawny bag of bones not fall after such bloodletting? Bhuvan may have given me my life back, but I certainly aided with his death. Did his mother not see my hand forcing her son's fate?

His mother continued to write to me. She wrote every Shree Panchami, because that was when her son was born. She wrote of obscure events in Bhuvan's childhood. 'Did you see the mark on my son's forehead?' she would write. 'I dropped a steel glass on his head when he was three. The poor child wouldn't stop crying for hours, crying because he had never seen blood. His father told him he had come unsealed and the morning's rice would spill from his head.' She wrote about how he fell ill when he was seven months old and wouldn't drink her milk anymore, until her breasts hung heavy with the rejected milk of motherhood and developed an infection, and how she had to pierce herself with cactus thorns to relieve the burden 'until my little Krishnaji cried for his mother's milk again'. She wrote about the time her husband went northwards to sell his merchandise and never returned. 'Perhaps tumbled down a ravine with his load. Stubborn as he was, he never learned how to carry a doko, and insisted upon balancing the bundle on his head, going up slippery stone steps to Rai villages. I always warned him it was too heavy but would he ever listen?' He wanted only the best for Bhuvan. And how could it escape Bhuvan's father that the villagers secretly despised his industry and whispered, 'what kind of a living does one make by selling printed cotton to unwitting Rais and Sherpas?' They were sad effigies of a life she would have wanted to live, with her husband, with her son. But that wasn't to be, can't you see? Who has an unfair share of the world's misery but the Nepali woman? Her husband came from a land she hadn't heard of, and her son died for a cause not addressed to her.

Then her letters became infrequent. I thought the old

woman must have run out of things to say. And how much longer and how much more love could she have for her son's killer? She still had to make a living somehow; exhuming figurines from her past and reliving her memories of them was insufficient sustenance. The village secretary wrote finally—I had gotten so used to his immaculate hand that I read well into the letter, confused at such a sudden turn in the mother's tone, until I realized that these were no longer her words transcribed by a sympathetic man, but the man himself.

He had a flair for burying pertinent information in a heap of jargonized evasion. 'The immortal martyr, alas, has lost his mother,' he wrote, 'it being my unfortunate duty to relay these darkest tidings to her "other son", as our mother was wont to call you.' She died walking between the school and the village gate named after her son, two edifices over which she had no claim except her attachment to her son's name. Bhuvan—the entire world!

It became unbearable to me, this news of her demise, as if the last remaining ties of blood that I knew had been severed cruelly, needlessly. While she was still alive in Okhaldhunga I could claim a strange solace; Bhuvan's face stayed well away from me. When I would be telling the story of my shattered hipbone to eager listeners—here at Pasalwalni's teashop, in the bazaar below, when a minister visited our village asked to see the local revolutionary hero— I tried hard to recall Bhuvan's face, but the task became increasingly difficult as his mother's letters piled up. His

faces became many, like the faces of children around me,
like the faces of adolescent boys in books, but never again
the dotted, pitted face in black and white that I had found
staring at me between fruits and fortified drinks.

I had lost Bhuvan's face during those few years. When
Bhuvan's mother died, like all martyrs' mothers do, Bhuvan
came floating back, right here, again—*this* close to my face,
dotted and pitted and the same scrawny smile, his face
clearly and hastily cut out of a group photo—a hand visibly
resting on the right shoulder, reminding there were more,
that he was much more, that he still was, beyond the village
secretary's letters and the scar on my waist.

A Christian missionary passed through Gairigaun not long
after Bhuvan's mother's death and he spoke of the messiah.
I asked him what a messiah is. The more he explained the
more of Bhuvan I found in his answers. I can't believe,
though, that one man can die for every man's sins; I can't
agree that a man who lived two thousand years ago will
today be capable of absolving every soul's crimes. But Bhuvan
had been my messiah and there was no doubt about it. Was
he not stretched out on the cot beside me, his hands falling
to the sides, his blood draining into me? When I woke up,
was he not vanished? And did he not resurrect among
fruits? And who killed him, but our common enemy arising
from the depths of ourselves; a ubiquitous enemy feeding

on our anger, despairs, hopes? And when he was shattered, did he not consecrate the ground he fell on? I know who the true messiah is, I said to the missionary. I have seen him, and I have seen his blood spill to give life to me—and also this guilt, this calling to redress my sin unto him. The missionary looked puzzled, he said I was blaspheming the name of Ishu, but Kaviraj—you know how anything foreign agitates him after his miserable stint in Oman, how he says he is better off carrying a plough in Gairigaun than wearing a tie to work in an office—he told the missionary to take his messiah-foolery elsewhere, 'Because we have enough gods already and they do not come with promises of medicine and money. And what if he could walk on water? Our god sleeps on beds of serpents, floating atop an endless sea, caressing Bhringu's footprint emblazoned on his chest.'

I wrote to the village secretary again, asking him if he knew of other men like me who corresponded with the mother. He said, No, but why don't you try the district party office. I wrote to the Okhaldhunga party office and waited for the answer. It takes ages for letters to reach anywhere, and even longer for the replies to arrive. Then there is the matter of the party officials who think they've done their duty towards all dead soldiers of the revolution and find queries like mine a nuisance.

If a man can sacrifice his life for another man, I thought, he must have had great dreams, greater aspirations; and who else but myself to bring them to fruition, with the same blood that he would have sweated. Letters came from everywhere: his friends who had now been given jobs in development projects, schools and civil service; some teachers, some customs agents in Birgunj, some keeping accounts for members of Parliament in Kathmandu, others still struggling as political fledglings within the party. I had hoped to recreate this giant—for he was a giant to me, his sacrifice, his deadness and martyrdom in a single towering heavenly swirl, not chopped and castrated like mine. I had hoped that through the letters I could reconstruct Bhuvan into a venerable martyr. But he had been ordinary, even more so than me.

When someone much weaker than you confronts a brute much stronger than you and fights to the death in defence of an ideal, something gives inside: you become a bit of a coward. Out of love towards humanity, if nothing else, an absurd bravado surfaces, propels you to take lashes on your back. And in that act is the promise of forgiveness towards yourself. But, what if somebody cheats you out of that act of charity towards your own soul?

I was furious that Bhuvan had tricked me. He was no giant, but an insignificant village boy. Even worse, he was weaker than I was. At least, even in the tumult of the revolution, I had had the guts to decide on my own—the letters spoke of how Bhuvan was less than that. He was painted a lackey of the lowest order; a hanger-on, a side-show, a lampoon without an ideological stance of his own, a mind emptied of courage, a coolie for borrowed conviction. He brought tea and carried papers and looked after the leaders' shoes as they crowded into a room to discuss the revolution. He laughed when better informed party cadres teased him; he was a party cadet but did not understand anything of the party literature.

He was an oaf, most letters told me—the ghost that had been raised in me and the village secretary was inflated and unreal. He was eager to please everyone—his march at the fore of the sloganeering crowd was merely an aspect of that need in him. Not a fervently patriotic son of the soil, Bhuvan was trying to impress me when he gave me his blood. I thought, The poor man must have had a tough time in Okhaldhunga, with his father's nose and skin, with his father's burden of printed Calcutta cotton and jeering crowd of local peers. Of course he would try to impress me; he would try to impress everyone right up to his sad end. And what did he get? Martyrdom for himself, misery for his mother and this burdensome guilt for me.

Now he comes, occasionally, in hours like this when I repeat his story, where I must relive the humiliation all over again. If I seem to lack the enthusiasm to discuss your party literature, my new comrades, or if you see disgust on my face when you wave that flag in my face, can you really blame me?

How can I help but be angry at him? How can I help but be angry at you?

THE GAME

It was a Saturday and, like every Saturday, Harihar had slept in and asked his wife Binita to bring his morning tea to bed. He had dozed off to sleep again when she stepped out to buy vegetables, but awoke when he heard Mangal shout his name from the carom game on the street under his window. Once down the stairs and out in the streets of Naya Bazar, the familiar smell of diesel fumes made his eyes smart and gave him a mild headache. But Harihar was satisfied with the holiday and he smiled inwardly. Saturday giddied him and everything took on a golden hue: it was a day for lazily stretching the hours, doing as little as a man could on his day off from his job.

Most of the gang was there—petty bureaucrats and restaurant owners, owners of fashion boutiques and wholesalers of electronics, neighbours and college buddies— gathered for the weekly game of carom. They put up small bets and teased each other loudly, traded more often in insults than they sank the carom pieces. Losers paid for tea, but sometimes a winner would also buy a round. Harihar counted himself the lucky one among his friends: married but unburdened yet with children, a steady government job with promotions and positions ahead of him, with a superior who was genuinely fond of him and goaded him onward to greater opportunities. He pushed files from one desk to the next, adding his initials against other initials to indicate he was in the know, occasionally went on field trips with expatriate consultants to represent the Health Ministry and nodded at villagers who asked him for favours from the foreigners. Every evening, he came home to Binita, who would have already cooked dinner, as if to shoo him into bed right away.

He won three games straight—the stakes were raised with every win because Mangal was not a graceful loser, and especially indignant whenever he lost to Harihar. Harihar pocketed the first two wins, modest by any comparison, tokens to spur on a friendly competition. With the third win he felt safely generous. Just to spite Mangal, Harihar bought a round of tea for everyone, Mangal included. After Mangal lost a few more rounds, he sourly tipped the board over and declared that everybody needed to go home to eat now. Harihar laughed and put his arms around Mangal's shoulders to give him a squeeze.

Sunidhi, the landlord's wife, was coming down the stairs. Harihar was whistling a tune and jumping a few steps at a time. He did not stop whistling as they passed. Sunidhi didn't even look in his direction. She huffed down the stairs and out. There had been raised voices upstairs the night before, but it had been followed by a long silence which had given way to the small sounds of lovemaking. Whenever Sunidhi's husband drank too much he hit her. Harihar knew that. He also knew that Sunidhi never fought about being hit, but only about the drinking. He wondered how much he was a part of Sunidhi's fate, but he also knew that he was in no place to do anything about it.

Binita cowered on the floor, huddled over an upturned platter. Rice was scattered everywhere. She must have tried to clean up—there was a small pile of rice scooped together. But the effort has been aborted. Binita looked up, wiped her eyes, grabbed the low seat by the open window and rested her head against the windowsill. Harihar stood by the bed and whistled to her. She straightened her back, but didn't turn around. He thought, She hasn't cooked lunch. He crouched by her side and touched her elbow. She recoiled. Harihar sat on the bed, wondering what he was allowed to ask, what he should say as the husband. He didn't want to fight Binita. He wanted her to go back to being happy, humming badly as she read magazines on the bed. The pressure cooker hissed and filled the room with the smell of burnt dal.

Harihar took the pressure cooker off the stove and dunked it into a bucket of water. Binita looked at his face with alarm as the hot pressure cooker screeched in rage, sending balls of hot water skidding away from it.

'Have you been crying?' Harihar asked.

'No.' Binita gathered the rice and searched for husks and dirt and pebbles. Harihar twisted open the pressure cooker's lid and put it on the ledge outside the window, from where it spread the smell of burnt dal to every house in the neighbourhood. It felt like an affront against oneself, like flying a flag to ask everybody to look at Harihar and Binita, at how quickly this marriage has soured, without any signposts along the way between happy conjugation and slow estrangement.

Not very long ago, Binita had surprised him at the Ministry. 'Why didn't you call ahead?' he had asked her, annoyed that he also had to play husband along with colleague and subordinate. Jyoti Prasad, the section officer, called Harihar to his office. Harihar started apologizing, saying he hadn't asked Binita to visit. Jyoti Prasad smiled and rapped the pen on his desk to get Harihar to shut up. 'Go,' he said, 'take the afternoon off. Show her the city.' Binita had been upset by the offhand manner in which Harihar had treated her in his office, so she had sulked through the day, only occasionally grunting at him when he haggled with a vendor for a mango or paused too long before movie posters. But Harihar had enjoyed that day. Binita laughed, eventually, when he made a fool of himself trying to eat with chopsticks in a Chinese restaurant. Her laugh changed the evening. He even pinched her cheeks in public. She blushed and elbowed him. Look at her now, balled up in a corner, gathering away from him anything that might spill from her, hiding from him the face he loved to watch as the smallest joy lit it up.

Binita quickly fried up some potatoes with green beans and boiled gundruk for a stew. Ground coriander and tomato chutney went well with the rice. She did not say anything to Harihar, but stared at his reflection on the glass of water, her chin propped on her right knee, her left ankle hooked behind the right. I did ask her if she was unhappy, Harihar thought. 'I will be back by four,' he told Binita after he finished eating. If she won't tell me what makes her so morose, he thought, why should I sit around and mope along with her?

Harihar wandered all the way from Naya Bazar to Putali Sadak. For a Saturday, there were too many people on the streets. 'There are too many people in this city,' he told an acquaintance whom he was meeting after four months. 'There is no other place to go to,' his acquaintance replied. The accuracy of the observation vexed Harihar a little, so he made up an excuse and left. A young man and a young woman had just finished painting fantastical figures on a wall near Bag Bazar. Harihar watched as the young woman took a stencil made out of an X-ray plate and signed the wall: a paint brush in an upraised fist. He walked on in a daze. In about an hour, he was forced to duck into a momo shop in Jyatha when he saw his acquaintance from earlier in the day approach him with a broad grin. He faced away from the street, ordered a plate of momos, and hoped the other man hadn't seen him. But his mind perked up: Perhaps they do see you, Harihar, all who scrutinize you for transgressions. How would you ever know if they know?

Harihar was in Thamel when a digital clock outside a bank blinked its row of big red lights to announce that it was four o'clock. Thamel was preparing for yet another street festival. Strings of light criss-crossed the narrow sky between crammed buildings. He wondered if he had enough money for a drink before heading home. He wanted to drink like an unfettered man. He wanted to look at women without shame or guilt. He walked up the stairs to a badly lit place but couldn't recognize any of the bottles behind the bar, except for the Johnny Walker, which he knew he couldn't afford.

In Naya Bazar he saw Sunidhi and crossed the street to greet her. She pretended to look at the tomatoes in a plastic bag she carried. Sunidhi and Binita were always together, passing bowls of curries between their two kitchens, buying matching saris, falling asleep through hot days in July as they chatted before the television. If anybody knew what was troubling Binita, it would be Sunidhi. Harihar wondered if he should ask her. But that will only make them happier, he thought, the two have their intestines entwined, and I know I haven't done anything wrong. Why should he apologize if he didn't know his offense? But he followed her around, not knowing what to say or do, until she, too, walked away in a huff.

He wanted to buy some whisky, something cheap after the shock of paying for a drink of Johnny Walker at the bar, but he bought meat instead. Saturday evenings were for meat. He carefully selected tomatoes and spring onions.

It was almost six when he finally reached home. Binita was in bed, a quilt pulled over her head. 'You shouldn't sleep in the evenings,' he said. 'Gives you a fever and makes you melancholy.' He handed her the meat. She did not even look at it. 'Make it hot, lots of chilli.' He rubbed his hands in mock glee.

He went upstairs to borrow the newspaper from Sunidhi. She hollered from her kitchen and told him where the paper was. When he returned, he found Binita working diligently. He felt successful when she threw garlic into the oil; the rich smell and sizzle of red onions and the thick mix of freshly ground cumin and coriander seeds filled the room. The newspaper carried stories about ministers convicted for corruption, suicide bombers in Chechnya, Lebanon, Palestine and Sri Lanka, industrial strikes in South Korea and Germany, executions in China, Yemen and Burundi, drug smugglers caught in Thailand, Singapore and Mexico, and a story about a serial rapist in the south of Pakistan. Binita quietly laid out one plate on the floor before the kerosene stove. 'Come on now,' Harihar half chided and half complained, 'we'll eat together tonight.'

Binita clanged the dishes when she cleaned them in a plastic bucket; her bangles chimed and she grunted as she scrubbed the pressure cooker; Harihar fell asleep without even taking off his shirt. She was gone when he woke up. He changed into his pyjamas and waited, but fell asleep again. She crept into bed silently and turned her back to him. He waited for a while before reaching out. She flinched under his touch, but he continued to trace pictures on her back. He wondered when he could reach for her breast. She sighed dispassionately. He gave up.

Sunday was a holiday, too, but the streets were just as crowded. 'Get dressed,' he told Binita. 'We should go to a temple somewhere. Somewhere you haven't been before.'

'Not today,' she said, 'it is one of the days.'

'Has it already been a month?' he asked. He thought he had learned to keep count of her days. He was disappointed. Sunidhi had drawn up a list of temples and deities for Binita. Any number of goddesses could bless a woman, and Sunidhi liked to dress Binita for the frequent trips to temples around the city. Bottles of mixes and Ayurvedic concoctions sent by her mother sat in a small box under the bed. Harihar's superiors at office gave him names of doctors and shamans.

Harihar went to the greengrocer's instead, and fought with the woman over the price of mustard leaves. He then went to the next grocer and bought squash and radishes, although he had really wanted to eat mustard leaves that evening. He had cooked for himself for six years before he married Binita, but now he had grown used to her cooking. During the first few months of their marriage Binita would praise him excessively over the six meals he had to cook over the three days of the month when she was impure. But his way of cooking meant his choice of vegetables—almost never anything of the season or economical, always insensible. He soon tired of it. He had once tried to persuade

Binita. 'It is an old and meaningless custom. You cook so much better than I do. Mother would never know, and no one else would have to know, anyway.' But Binita had talked to Sunidhi about it, and Sunidhi had descended upon him for suggesting something so vile and unorthodox. 'You men become so easily godless when it is your turn to move a fallen twig,' she had said. 'If you can't do it, I'll cook for us all,' Sunidhi had offered, perhaps knowing well that it would force Harihar to submit to tradition.

Binita was still silent as she did the morning's dishes, of which there was more than the usual clutter. Harihar considered raising his voice to demand an explanation about her silence, but that would create a needless argument. After an hour of pretending to look out of the window and thumbing through the three photo albums they had acquired since their marriage, he told Binita that he would be back by four. She looked at him with trembling lips. 'I said I will be back.' He shook his head at her.

'Why is Binita not speaking to me?' he asked Sunidhi when he ran into her on the street.

'Is she your wife or mine?' she retorted.

'What did I do?' Harihar asked. 'Now you are angry at me too! What did I do?' He looked at Sunidhi's face. For some odd reason he thought of a poster for a Hindi movie— the number-one heroine of Indian cinema showed her navel and wore very pointed bras. Harihar blushed and glanced up at his window, worried if Binita was watching them. Sunidhi followed his gaze and snorted before rushing homeward. He thought he heard Sunidhi mutter something. Did she say, 'What sort of a husband are you?'

Harihar jumped into a crowded bus to Balaju. Floating amidst the various odours of the bodies around him, he hung from the strap and thought about Sunidhi's comment. Why should she say that? The longer he pondered, the more he was convinced that she had said that not about him, but about her own husband.

Perhaps she had glanced up at her own window, directly above Harihar's window. After all, she was wearing the scarf again to hide the bruises on her neck. And now that he thought of it, he knew she was out to buy alcohol for her husband. When the bus turned left on Chakrapath, Harihar realized he had taken the wrong bus. He shouted at the conductor and tried to pay only ten rupees instead of fifteen, but other passengers started yelling at him for the hold-up. He decided he would walk the rest of the way—after all, he had made a mistake; he might as well pay for it.

He was sweating by the time he reached the Asta Narayan Cinema Hall. A woman wore a dress that showed off her back. Harihar stood behind her on the ticket line. The woman's back was covered in the fine dark scars of the pimples that had once plagued her. An hour into the movie, Harihar realized that he hadn't been following the story. He could not remember who had killed the heroine's mother. He tried to ask the schoolboy sitting next to him, but the boy was incoherent with excitement. Then the movie burst into a song-and-dance routine. It would be nicer with Binita, he thought. He felt bad about the ticket money which would have sufficed for the evening's greens. Bitter gourd, perhaps—Binita would enjoy it, too, and wasn't it supposed to be good for young couples?

A man rushing down brushed past Harihar as he climbed the stairs to his room. Harihar thought there was something familiar about him, but couldn't quite place the face, couldn't decide where he had met him. Sunidhi stood at the top of the stairs. 'Who was that?' Harihar asked her.

'My nephew,' Sunidhi said, and disappeared.

Binita was at the window, but she turned sharply when Harihar entered the room.

'Expecting someone else?' he teased.

'Shameless!' she said.

He made tea for her. She was still sulking. Harihar asked Binita the usual questions, but that did not change anything. Monday seemed to thaw her a little, Tuesday was better.

When she could touch fire again on Wednesday, she made fried potatoes and two kinds of chutney in the morning; there was plenty left over but when Harihar returned in the evening it was all gone. When he praised the morning's potatoes, she made the dish again, chattering all the while, asking him if she could visit her brother on Saturday. 'We will go together,' he told her. Her face clouded instantly. The potatoes did not turn out as good.

He touched her waist and traced the contour of her hip as he tried to fight the slumber induced by rice. He turned her over. She crossed her legs and said she had cramps. It is especially bad this time, she said. Thursday was no different. On Friday night he came home drunk and slapped her once, regretted it, and stormed out. He was sober when he returned just before dawn, after stumbling around the temples of Pashupatinath where he sat beside large bonfires and laughed himself silly with the sadhus.

Saturday morning was as usual. Mangal won the first game and it was difficult to get him to shut up. Harihar talked about the temples and how he had seen the strangest sadhus. 'Bed not warm enough for you?' Mangal said, and made everyone laugh.

'Looks like the cooking pot hasn't simmered for a while,' Jyoti Prasad said. He wasn't just the oldest man in the group, but also the highest-ranked government official among the petty clerks around the carom board. Harihar concentrated hard on netting the red queen because Mangal was down to his last two discs.

A convoy of Indian trucks carrying goats was stuck between two large landslides on the road along the Trishuli River. Mutton was temporarily very expensive. Binita was making chicken for lunch instead. Before he left for his carom game, Harihar had tried to think of things to say to her, but could not concentrate for long enough to string together the kind of careful phrases he thought he would need to speak to Binita. Harihar lost again after failing to capitalize on an early lead. 'I can't concentrate,' he said. 'Any excuse a loser makes is a good enough excuse,' Mangal said. Harihar struck the queen with a little too much force. Instead of falling into the pocket, the striker and the queen bounded off the far side of the board. 'Our man is having trouble finding the hole,' Mangal quipped.

Harihar's head hurt as he entered the room after the game. The rice was kept warm by the rice cooker, the pressure cooker was still on the stove, and the smell of a ready meal permeated the room. He could hear Sunidhi walking in her kitchen upstairs. He read a new novel by one of his colleagues while he waited for Binita to return. It was about a village near Pokhara, of generations of the same family caught in a vortex of different kinds of violence. It started with the settlement of the valley by two brothers whose descendants turned into bitter enemies, and finished with the consequences in the village of the first Iraqi invasion by the Americans. It was a bad novel. When he felt a sudden pang of pain and realized how hungry he was, he knocked on Sunidhi's door. Sunidhi wasn't wearing the scarf, but she still looked unhappy.

'Is Binita inside?' he asked.

'No.'

'I thought she was watching TV with you.'

'I haven't seen her since morning.'

Harihar felt foolish and left abruptly. He thought he heard Sunidhi mutter something behind his back, but Sunidhi usually muttered something or the other. Only when he was back on the bed did he realize he had forgotten to ask Sunidhi if she knew where Binita might have gone off to. But it seemed even more foolish to sit by himself. He walked upstairs again. 'Do you know where she might be?' he asked.

Sunidhi wiped her hands and constantly turned towards the kitchen where something might be burning. 'You really don't know, do you?' Sunidhi scratched her neck.

'Know what?' Harihar felt foolish again.

'About where Binita went?'

'She has been sulking for a while, but it was because she wanted to go visit her brother's family today. I told her I would take her.'

Sunidhi looked at him with pity. Harihar did not like it. 'Why are you looking at me like that?' he asked. Her husband beats her every night, but she has pity for other people who don't even need it. The irony of it, he thought.

'You are a simple man, Harihar.' Sunidhi stepped back through the door.

Harihar climbed down the stairs and served himself a large helping of rice and chicken. He ate more than usual and then took a short nap. He dreamed of a woman he could not name and woke up very thirsty.

There was much life in the streets. The city was preparing for Krishna Janmasthami. Children would be adorned with peacock feathers and flutes to play the infant Krishna, mothers would coo over their sons, fathers would put babies on their shoulders and walk through the throng of lights and music and frenzied chants of devotion. Binita returned around four in the afternoon. Harihar had just awoken and was looking out of the window, at nothing in particular. A man wearing a baseball cap walked Binita home, turning away sharply before the door. Harihar couldn't see the man's face, but the gait seemed familiar.

'He is Bhauju's brother,' Binita explained later in the evening, startled that Harihar had seen them. 'Brother thought it would be difficult for me to get here, what with the crowd in the streets.'

'I thought I had seen him before,' Harihar said. He scolded Binita for not inviting Bhauju's brother up for tea. 'What is his name?' he asked.

'Why do you need it?' Binita suddenly sounded very testy. Harihar glared at her. 'Navin,' she said finally, looking Harihar in the eye.

It was a Wednesday evening. The monsoon showers had ceased. Binita was not home so Harihar made himself some tea and sat by the window. Sunidhi's husband came around the corner, already staggering. Harihar ran down to help carry the drunkard. Sunidhi did not meet his eyes when she opened the door. Her husband brushed her aside, walked a few paces and fell on his face.

Harihar waited for Sunidhi's husband to quiet down before asking about Binita. Sunidhi opened the door, keeping one eye on the kitchen door and one eye on Harihar. 'Did she mention anything to you?' Harihar asked.

'She must have gone to her brother's place in Jawalakhel. Doesn't she always go there?'

'Yes,' Harihar said. It was awkward to stand there for too long. Sunidhi's husband stirred inside, so Harihar returned to his room. The earthen pot in which Binita aged rice was almost empty. The tin pot for lentils was full. There were enough spices in the rack, and more in glass jars above the kerosene stove. Binita had misplaced the funnel; Harihar poured kerosene into the stove directly from the can, spilling some on his hands and shoes.

Dishes were arranged differently from how he normally arranged them. There was a new set of tea cups and saucers that he had never noticed before. A grocery list written in Binita's hand was inside a jar of dried chilli pods. The rice turned out watery. He forgot to put salt into the potatoes that smelled of kerosene. He chopped up coriander to sprinkle on the curry, but forgot until the very last morsel. Binita did not return that night.

'Why haven't you shaved, Harihar?' Jyoti Prasad asked the next afternoon, circling in red ink the errors in the file Harihar had submitted earlier. 'Turning ascetic, are we, Harihar? This is a government office. Clerks, officers—everyone must be in tip-top shape, presentable before public. Difficult to move to the top without proper decorum. Must have ambition and attitude.' Harihar said he was sick and needed to leave early. Jyoti Prasad cocked his head and looked at Harihar. He came to Harihar's desk after fifteen minutes and told him to leave if he needed.

He was in Jawalakhel within an hour, but had no luck there either. 'You are the husband. If you don't know, how would I?' said Binita's brother, not bothering to drink the tea going cold before him. 'The day I gave her to you in marriage I asked for your promise to look after her, keep her happy in every possible way. If the pot cracks, you must plaster it together. I can only weep for her misfortunes, but you have to find your own happiness,' he said. Binita had not been to Jawalakhel in six months. The first bright stars dripped into the night outside. Twenty yards from the gate, when Harihar turned to look at Binita's brother, he saw the man's shoulders sag under an immense burden.

By the second evening, he was already cooking enough to have leftover food for the morning. On the fourth day, he noticed that she hadn't yet cleaned some of her clothes; her smell occupied a corner. He found a list of relatives and friends—his close acquaintances, all thirteen of them, and her friends from the brief stint at Padma Kanya Campus, the women's college, five women. Binita must have used the list to invite their relatives and friends over on the few occasions they had been able to entertain. He realized that the list could come handy eventually, when she would decide to end her sulking. Harihar had to wear the same shirt twice by the time Friday came around. He did not shave the entire week.

Sunidhi frightened him, too—if he saw her in the distance,

he would step into a shop or an alley. Instead of drinking, he went browsing for second-hand books in Sundhara. On Saturday morning, he washed his shirts and trousers under the tap and asked Sunidhi if he could dry them on the roof. 'You should have told me,' she said, 'I would have washed them.' She wouldn't let him put the laundry on the lines. 'What will the neighbours say if they see you? It makes me look rude, as if I can't take care of you in this hour of need.'

Sunidhi's husband knocked on the door in the evening. 'How is the bachelor life?' he asked. He smelled of alcohol. The piece of newspaper wrapped around the bottle of vodka had a poem about a waterfall in eastern Nepal. 'Electricity water!' said Sunidhi's husband. 'It cures any ailment. Except women. They are an incurable disease. Man's predicament, if you ask me, he willingly infects himself then rues for remainder life. Not original thought, some poet somewhere.'

'Except women!' Harihar slapped Sunidhi's husband's back cheerily. They stuck their head out of the window and called Sunidhi. She went to Gokul's restaurant for fried goat offal with chopped onion and raw garlic.

'Except women,' said Sunidhi's husband after they finished half of the bottle.

'But you have an excellent woman for a wife,' Harihar said.

'Who is talking about this woman?' Sunidhi's husband laughed. Sunidhi laughed with him. 'Bless this woman's heart,' her husband said as he grabbed her waist and made her sit on his lap for a few seconds before she squirmed out of reach again, 'she is very understanding.'

On Sunday afternoon, Mangal knocked to ask Harihar to join the other men around the carom board. 'You are in a bad shape,' he said and sat by the window. The other men occasionally glanced up at them. Harihar waved to the men, but did not go downstairs.

On Tuesday evening, Sunidhi's husband made him shave. 'You need to look respectable for where we are going,' he said with a wink. He took Harihar to a house by Gopi Krishna Cinema in Chabahil. When Jyoti Prasad commented on his absent stubble the next morning, Harihar touched his chin and realized that on the night before, he had chosen a woman who looked just like Sunidhi. He wondered if Sunidhi's husband had seen through the game. 'You don't have to be shy with me, Harihar,' Sunidhi's husband had commented. 'We are equals down there.'

Jyoti Prasad called Harihar to his office on Thursday. 'If you think you will use the day wisely,' he said, 'I think you should spend tomorrow towards some good end. I have heard that you still don't know where Binita is. It isn't good to be so apathetic. After all, you are her husband.'

'Hariharji!' someone called as Harihar signed for the next few days in the roster by the office entrance. It was Navin, Bhauju's nephew. Harihar searched behind Navin, hoping that perhaps he had brought Binita to him, like he had done before. Navin turned around, too, and faced Harihar with the downturned, worn smile of a brow-beaten jester.

'I'm sure you've heard Binita isn't home,' said Harihar. 'I didn't go to the police or to the hospitals. I don't have the guts to do either. I just don't seem to think anything has happened to her.' Navin simply looked out of the bus window. He had agreed to come home with Harihar after he pressed Navin to keep him company for the evening. Women wore red in anticipation of Dashain. The streets were sparse—people who thronged the streets all year long disappeared into the folds of the mountains or dispersed into the plains in the south as the festivals called them home. The empty streets of Kathmandu lamented the absence of the teeming humanity that otherwise gave it its rotten urban texture. 'Everybody has a place to go,' Harihar said. 'But I only have an empty room to sleep in.' Navin fidgeted in his seat.

At home, Sunidhi's husband arranged the bottle and glasses and plates of meat on newspaper sheets laid on the floor. 'I don't think I want to drink,' Navin said, glancing at the bed and the stove and the walls. Binita's clothes were still in the corner where she had left them. Sunidhi briskly bundled everything up to unceremoniously stuff them under the bed. Harihar didn't like that, but he didn't stop Sunidhi either.

'Are you sure you don't know where Binita went?' Sunidhi

asked, pouring Navin some vodka. Navin looked at her as if
stunned, then gulped down the vodka and wiped his
forehead. Sunidhi poured vodka for her husband and
Harihar, shuffling crablike across the room. She watched
the men from a corner. Harihar thought he saw her scowl
at Navin.

'Dhat!' Harihar said, tearing a piece from the newspaper
to wipe off the grease on his fingers. 'What did I do to that
woman? I slapped her once, just once in three years, and
she runs away.'

'She'll come back, Harihar. Just you wait, she'll come
back,' Sunidhi's husband said.

Harihar couldn't drink the vodka fast enough to gather
the courage he needed to ask Sunidhi and Navin a question
that was rattling in his head, bulging his eyes out of their
sockets. He quickly drank four glasses of vodka, and when
he felt the tongue slur and his face flush hot and red, he
pointed a finger at Sunidhi and wagged it. 'You told me
that he,' now Harihar wagged at Navin, 'that he was your
nephew. You said that, didn't you?'

Sunidhi and Navin looked at each other, frightened.
Harihar cuffed Navin's head, without malice. 'You were
wearing a cap, running down the stairs.' Sunidhi's husband
flared his nose and glared at Sunidhi, who simply turned
away. Navin looked at the floor. After an awkward moment
Sunidhi started ladling meat to the men. She poured more
vodka for Navin and pushed it into his hands.

'And now you say you are Bhauju's brother!' Harihar
growled.

After draining clean the glass Sunidhi handed him, Navin turned to Harihar. 'I am not Binita's relative,' he said, 'I am her lover.' Harihar picked the biggest piece of meat from his saucer and started chewing the gristly lump.

'She sent me to tell you that she wants to come back,' Navin said. Harihar chewed on another piece of meat. The sort of silence that seems to beg for an explanation animated Sunidhi's husband. He lamented how he couldn't call Binita any names, because, after all, she was a wonderful woman. But he said, Who am I to blame anyone? I am the worst human being I know. Sunidhi slapped his wrist lightly. 'Shouldn't say such inauspicious things,' she scolded him.

'But you never know—don't you see?' her husband replied. 'You can never tell what people will turn into. Perfectly nice today, but tomorrow they'll stick a knife in your back.'

Harihar jumped up, stuck his head out of the window, and retched. It wasn't the alcohol, because he knew he could drink more in an evening. It couldn't have been the meat, because Harihar could stomach half a kilo of it before the first burp came. He hadn't felt sick; the air was balmy and cool. He had even been enjoying the evening in a melancholy, morbid way. Sunidhi's husband held his shoulders.

Navin stood to go. He said, 'Binita says she wants to come back.' Harihar wiped his mouth and unbuttoned his shirt, exposing his chest and soft belly. His head was clearer now. He sat down and bit into another piece of meat. Sunidhi tried to take the bottle away, but her husband said

Harihar would be fine, let him have more. She sat by her husband and took a piece of meat from his saucer.

Harihar picked at the garnish, unable to meet Navin's eyes. 'What should I tell her?' Navin asked from the door. His face was flushed.

'You don't have to go quite yet,' Harihar said.

'I think I should,' Navin said.

'Now, sit down when the man asks you.' Sunidhi's husband grabbed Navin by his wrist. 'A little bit of electricity water fixes everything.' Navin looked to Sunidhi, as if for her permission. When Sunidhi's husband waved him over impatiently, he promptly sat back down.

'On that day, I came here to beg her to leave you.' Navin tried to land his glass of vodka on the wet ring it left on the newspaper on the floor. 'I kept begging her. That was the only way I knew. But when she came with me, it was difficult to show her that I loved her enough. I tried very hard.'

'Does she ever talk about me?' Harihar asked.

Binita talked about Harihar all the time. How Navin had been able to fend off jealousy for so long, Navin did not know. Harihar shouldn't be jealous of Navin either. Harihar saw the tears in Navin's eyes and started sniffling along with Navin. That got Sunidhi and her husband in stitches, holding their bellies as they laughed, pointing at Navin, pointing at Harihar.

Harihar shaved on Friday morning. He dug out the aftershave that had come as a wedding present. Sunidhi took his shirt and trousers upstairs and pressed them for him. He wanted to wear them in the morning, but Sunidhi's husband wouldn't let him. Sunidhi cleaned Harihar's room. Her husband helped Harihar move the bed to a different spot. Harihar cleaned the grime off the stove, rearranged the spices and dry food, and bought a new bag of rice and a second-hand black-and-white TV. Sunidhi's husband borrowed a length of coaxial wire to steal signal from his own set. Looking at the freshly cleaned and arranged room, Harihar felt like a new bride.

Navin came around the corner exactly at four. He stopped and called out to Binita. She came around the corner and hesitated, then glanced at the window. I shouldn't have waited by the window, Harihar thought, and hoped the new curtains hid him well. Sunidhi and her husband must be at their window. Binita grabbed Navin's arm, but he pried his arm free and looked up. He walked back to the corner, put a cigarette in his mouth and patted his pockets. Binita looked at him, but he turned away and walked further. Binita disappeared under the awning of the house. Harihar could hear her footsteps on the stairs. He opened the curtain wide and stuck his head out. Navin waved at him, the unlit cigarette dangling from his lips, and disappeared around the corner, still patting his pockets.

STAMP AND SIGNATURE

It wasn't much of a plot, but it seemed affordable to Sunil. A track, four metres wide, branched from the main artery of the housing plan, turned a corner to touch three other plots, and ended here. The line of bare concrete utility poles along the track terminated just outside the property limits. The hills to the north were barely a half-kilometre away; water sourced directly from springs in the hills would always be plentiful. Although the place was far from the centre of Kathmandu, a microbus route passed through the housing plan, tin boxes full of limbs hurtling past every fifteen minutes. With the savings that would naturally occur after the family moved into its own property, a scooter wouldn't be too ambitious a dream, either. Sunil had saved enough over the years to be able to put down two-thirds of the money the seller demanded. His wife, Nirmala, had her savings, but he wouldn't ask her. Let her hold on to it, he thought, I'll build the house, she'll put in the curtains.

Sunil stood in the middle of the empty plot and measured

it with his eyes. That's where the main door will be, he thought, and that will be the living room. Through, and to the right, will be the kitchen. Nirmala will stand in that corner, watching the tea boil on the gas stove, serene and silent without the fiery hiss of the kerosene stove. Across the kitchen, in another corner, Nanu will open the fridge to check if Nirmala's cream-and-coconut confection has frozen into an ice-lolly. Nanu won't have a yard to run around in, but that won't matter—there'll be the roof, after all, and Nanu won't remain a child for very long. To the left of the living room will be my room, with a door leading to a narrow perch outside, where I'll sit with my newspaper. A weed with clusters of yellow flowers grew on the spot. Sunil walked up to the weed and pulled it out. The flowers became a yellow mush and lodged under his nails.

'What do you think, then?' Thapa, the realtor, asked, clutching a black diary under his arm. Sunil wiped his fingers on a handkerchief and looked at the horizon to the west.

The television flickered like a wick in the wind and lit up Nanu's face as she slept on a mat before it. From the bed, Nirmala changed the channel restlessly and fidgeted. Sunil nudged closer to her hair.

'I went to see the plot,' he half whispered. 'It's just big enough for us.'

'What did Hari dai say?' Nirmala asked. Sunil had visited his elder brother before coming home in the evening.

'Nothing. He just read the newspaper from the morning. Bhauju talked for the both of them. She never mentioned the land in the village.' Nirmala fidgeted again, then switched off the television. She turned to Sunil.

'We can't use your money,' Sunil said after a moment. Nirmala massaged his palm. 'But we could use it to repay a loan, just the instalments,' she said. He touched her hair and traced the outlines of her ear, the soft earlobe and the ridge of the brows. A cool breeze shook the curtains and entered the room like a blessing. Nirmala kissed his hand. 'You worry too much,' she said, 'let me worry with you.' She snuggled closer into his arms. Sunil waited for her to fall asleep, but it took a long hour before she dozed off.

The next evening, Sunil visited the plot again, alone. He wanted to avoid Thapa and look at the plot again in the comfort of solitude. But, just as he was leaving, Thapa walked towards him, grinning broadly. Sunil felt trapped. An aged man with a worn umbrella followed Thapa. Sunil could tell from the sweat-stained kurta and battered leather shoes that the man wasn't from the city.

'Sir here is a party worker from the district,' Thapa introduced the aged man.

'I am only a farmer,' said the man humbly, and joined his hands in a namaste. 'I am Shila Nath Arjel.'

'He is with the Ministry.' Thapa pointed to Sunil, baring his gums and sending his black diary to its sweat-drenched station under his arm. 'Powerful man, this Sunil babu,' he said.

'What power, Thapa dai?' Sunil greeted Arjel with a namaste. 'I am a stamp-signature man. What power does a clerk have in these times?'

A cloud blocked the sun. It brought some relief from the glare and the heat, but also made Sunil uneasy about this chance meeting with Thapa. Without the sun the hills seemed to loom closer, faraway objects lost their sharp outlines, and the world seemed murkier, uncertain. Thapa broke the silence. 'Arjel sir is also thinking of buying this plot, Sunil babu. With neighbours like you—either of you—I am tempted to buy the next plot and settle my family here.'

Sunil looked in Arjel's direction, but the old man was grinding his teeth as he squinted at the small plot of land. Sunil waited to see if Arjel's face would betray any of his dreams for the house he'd perhaps build, snatching the land away from Sunil.

That night Sunil looked at Nirmala with sad eyes, but played with his daughter more cheerfully than he usually did. Maya didi from the adjacent room brought a bowl of goat curry, meat from a sacrifice she'd given at the Manakamana temple where supplicants exchange blood for boons. She didn't linger. Her niece peeled Nanu away from the television so that they could go to Maya didi's room to play with the new puzzle book she'd brought home from school. Nirmala busied herself by the stove. Sunil sat before the television, mesmerized but not watching.

A tourist couple held hands and walked happily through the dirty crowd in Thamel. They laughed at the albino sarangi-seller who conjured phrases in their languages as he strummed his instrument and played snatches of folk tunes—'Resham firiri', 'Paan ko paat'—which also filtered in from the thumping big amplifiers in music shops. The tourist woman stopped to examine a clever incense-holder in the shape of a fat laughing Buddha. His gaping, laughing mouth let out a continuous wisp of fragrant smoke. When her partner tried to pull her away, she patted his belly and laughed, pointing at the incense-holder.

Thousands of kilometres from home, thought Sunil, and look how carefree they are, how happy. But they have money enough to travel, and surely they have a house of their own back where they come from. And, this couple probably doesn't have children. They are probably not even married to each other. Who knows? Maybe they met just the other day, here in Thamel, and started holding hands. They are together only as long as it is good being together. Jealousy blanketed his heart. He returned the cup to the tea-seller and counted the change in his pockets.

'Namaste, Sunil babu!' Somebody touched his elbow. It was Arjel, with his umbrella hanging from the crook of his arm.

'Namaste, sir,' Sunil said. He could see that Arjel was just as disturbed by this chance encounter. Arjel looked at the stale confectionaries on the tea-seller's cart and turned away towards the Sanchaya Kosh office. 'You are from here,' Arjel started, 'but I am still a stranger in Kathmandu. It is hard to find my way around the city. Even harder to find my way in there.' He pointed at Sanchaya Kosh. 'At least you know your way around bureaucracy,' he said.

'I'm not from around here either,' said Sunil. They ambled, shoulder to shoulder, towards Sanchaya Kosh. The crowd outside the office was subdued, on the verge of dejection, but resilient. Sanchaya Kosh was the keeper of government employees' provident funds. Officers inside could decide how much money you were eligible to draw in loans. They could decide whether or not a clerk or a teacher could afford the coveted new piece of land. A woman rushed out, gesticulating wildly, wiping her teary eyes. 'You people think I am powerless,' she shouted. 'I'll ring you up from Singha Durbar, from the Minister's mobile phone! I have reach. I have people in high places. I have fed them with these hands!' She fumed outside Sanchaya Kosh for five minutes. Nobody spoke to her or met her eyes. She rushed in again, perhaps to plead her case one last time. Perhaps she was turned down yet again—she came out, deflated, her face in ruins, her arsenal of threats now empty. She tried to hail a taxi, but in her humiliation and fury, she seemed to have forgotten than she was standing on the wrong side of the street. She waited, wiping her eyes with a dark shawl.

Of course Sunil knew, but he still gathered courage and asked Arjel, 'What brings you here, sir?'

'Have you been looking at other plots, Sunil babu?' Arjel sir asked. 'You live here. You must have seen other plots like that.'

'I never had the courage to look for land before this,' Sunil said. I shouldn't have to open my heart to anybody, he thought, humiliated by his confession to Arjel sir.

'I am a poor man from the hills, Sunil babu. I teach at the local high school, and I work what little land I have. This plot I can afford only if I sell land in the village and get a good loan from Sanchaya Kosh.'

Sunil felt something knot up inside: a ball of air, a fist of anxiety—not a physical sensation, but nausea stuck to the inside of his chest. He couldn't afford to lose this plot. He had to put together the money he needed, no matter what it took. Perhaps Nirmala could go to Hari dai, take Nanu with her, and talk about the land in the village. It was a tricky situation. The land remaining in the ancestral village was registered under Hari dai's name, and Hari dai refused to sell it to help Sunil in this hour of his need. He also refused to give Sunil a loan. Perhaps Nirmala could melt Bhauju's heart, and Bhauju could then harass Hari dai into giving Sunil a loan. Who would they turn to at such a time, if not family?

'But that's not a very good plot,' said Arjel suddenly. 'Sitting at the forest edge, littered with jackal turds. So far from the city, so far from hospitals. What would anyone do in case of an emergency?'

'And the river nearby?' Sunil felt the obligation to add fuel to this fire. 'It is an open sewer, that's what it is. Wait till the place is full of houses. Where will the sewers go?' Arjel fidgeted with his umbrella, but kept his eyes fixed on a shiny object far away. He reminded Sunil of men from his village, old uncles he had grown up around—honest farmers, men of honour and courtesy in their villages, men who'd be baffled by Kathmandu and its crude ways.

'Do you have daughters?' Sunil asked. Arjel shot him a look. 'I have a daughter,' Sunil explained. 'She is only six. Very bright in school, but very timid. I'm worried what kind of a neighbourhood it will be for my daughter by the time she grows up.'

'Not a very good neighbourhood, Sunil babu,' Arjel muttered.

They waited their turn to push their files from desk to desk, but their turn never came. Later that evening, Sunil bought Arjel a cup of tea, and Arjel bought the samosas to go with it. They had walked to Bag Bazaar together, from where they'd get on separate city buses.

'It is all politics, Sunil babu,' Arjel said. 'I will go to Dhungel, the CA member from our area. I taught him, he passed SLC only after taking tuitions with me. He has reach, all the way up. I helped him during the decade, and during the elections. Dhungel will have to give me source-force. These stamp-signature people only understand source-force.'

Sunil flinched. Arjel must have realized his mistake, but

avoided acknowledging it. He sipped his tea, trying to suck the film of milk-clot from the surface. If Arjel said his source-force came from Dhungel, that was a powerful source-force to have to go up against. 'I will use source-force for both of us, Sunil babu. You don't worry. I will make calls, all the way up if I have to. If we can't live peacefully in Kathmandu city, where can we?'

But when Sunil met Arjel and Thapa at the plot three days later, Arjel seemed to have aged. His worn umbrella looked even more faded. Sunil watched as Arjel tried to close it, but it wouldn't stay shut. Thapa took the umbrella and tied it with a sash.

'Nothing came of it, Sunil babu,' Arjel cried. 'All of these big people—why would they listen to me? Their assistants pretend not to know me. Curs. My wife has cooked for them, fed them with her own hands.'

Houses of all shapes, colours and sizes dotted the riverbank, where land was cheapest. Laundry dried on rooftops. Carefully selected flowers in pots arranged along the edge of the roof or the outdoor staircase leading to the roof made even the poorest of the houses look like a procession of brides. A woman walked past a window, drawing shut the curtain without even looking out. Sunil read the houses and was mildly taken by jealousy.

'I say,' Thapa said in a deliberate drawl. 'I say, you two

should pitch in together to buy this land. Build a house together, share it.'

'It is a nice idea, Thapa dai,' Sunil said. He didn't want to be the one to throw water on such an idealistic proposition.

'It is a nice idea, Thapaji, but what is real is real. We can't both buy the same piece of land. I will try to use my source-force for both us,' Arjel said, but without any conviction. 'You don't lose heart yet, Sunil babu.'

Once more, Arjel and Sunil stood around listlessly, measuring the plot with their eyes, occasionally muttering under their breath, while Thapa wrung his hands and opened and shut his black diary. He made an excuse and left on his motorbike. Arjel and Sunil walked to the road from where they could catch microbuses back to the city.

Arjel wouldn't stop talking on the ride back. He told of his son who had just finished his high school exams and now wanted to go to Korea. '"Forget building a house in Kathmandu," he says to me every chance he gets,' Arjel said. 'But my wife is ill, weak and can hardly breathe when she cooks. I want her close to the hospitals, if something happens, you know. She is in the Teaching Hospital these days. It pains me to leave her there, in that cloud of phenyl fumes. The nurses are rude, and there is so much dying around her, left and right. Just this morning the woman next to her bed died in her sleep. What did the nurses do? They changed the sheets on the bed.'

Mallaji had shown himself into Sunil's office by the time he reached the Ministry. Sunil greeted Mallaji and went about his meagre daily ritual—unlock the drawers, arrange the stamps and ink pad on the table before him. Mallaji purred contentedly in the chair by the window.

Mallaji played with the thick gold ring on the fourth finger of his right hand. Each of Mallaji's fingers sported a unique ring—different metals, different stones, all according to strict astrological formulas. His rings clicked on the table as he hummed along to an old-fashioned song that drifted in from the teashop by the Ministry gate. Mallaji had pushed his sunglasses over his well-oiled hair. Sunil could see oil on Mallaji's fingertips, on the glasses, and the smears on the table. Mallaji wiped his fingers on his thick, luxurious moustache that covered his mouth and played with the thick gold chain that ringed his thick neck, separating the lustrous growth of chest hair from the jowly, chinless face. Mallaji ran a hotel in Thamel—no, not *that* one, but an obscure little establishment closer to Paknajol, on the western fringes of the tourist district. He needed Sunil's help in putting in a swimming pool in his hotel.

'Good for business, you know,' Mallaji said and looked out of the window. 'You see, Sunilji,' Malla started. He had the cockiness of someone who thought of himself as self-made, and therefore a know-it-all. 'When things go bad, they go bad in threes, always. Always. First it was the hijacking by neighbourhood terrorists, taking the plane to Afghanistan, killing people, what not. Then the local variety terrorism started—extortion, explosion, execution. Then international variety terrorism in New York spooked American backpackers, scared Israeli backpackers. Sunilji, before they would terrorize us poor businessmen with paper and pen, now they have hand-made pistols. If they kill businessmen they kill business; if they kill business they kill businessmen. But these riff-raff revolutionaries don't understand that, do they? Everybody looks at us and says, "You are making money, living in a nice house. Give us a little or we'll throw a bomb in your house." Government pressurizes us with VAT bills and income tax raids, Maoists terrorize us with pressure-cooker bombs. Business is totally dead, Sunilji. Only this swimming pool will revive it. This is the only elixir to my livelihood, Sunilji, please look at the file with a soft heart and approve it.'

'But it is a lot of water, Mallaji!' Sunil feigned protest and leaned back in his chair, dismissing the piece of paper Mallaji handed to him discreetly. It carried the figures Mallaji wanted Sunil to fill into the file before him. 'It says in clear red ink how much water your hotel buys. It should be enough to give hot and cold running water in every room. You are asking for a lot more.'

'Of course it is! This pool is my begging bowl, so to speak. Even businessmen have to eat, you know.' Mallaji leaned back and laughed, slapped his thigh and scratched his nose.

'You make cruel jokes, Mallaji,' Sunil said, opening Mallaji's file, perfunctorily reading the application and the figures on the form. 'You have such a grand hotel. I've seen it from the street. Even your tiffin is chef-prepared. Every room is air-conditioned, full of dollar-spending foreigners. And you call that a begging bowl!'

'Harey, Sunilji!' Mallaji sighed. 'I'm not asking for too much, am I? It's a simple change of projection, a slip of the pen, that's all. One hand won't know what the other did. Who doesn't make mistakes every now and then?'

'Your swimming pool will leave a hundred households cutting each other's throats. You don't know how it is to fight your neighbours every morning, do you, Mallaji?'

'This is Kali Yug, Sunilji.' The ominous phrase appeared. 'And this is democracy. People's rule—your rule, my rule. Who has lived happy by always being good? I have very powerful rivals, people with lot more muscle in politics. Poor man like me, what can I do but come and beg friends like you? How will you turn down a poor man's plea?'

Sunil's hand had unconsciously reached for the stamp even as he listened to Mallaji, minutely watching the hotelier's performance. Mallaji smiled under his moustache; his eyes went from Sunil's face to the stamp and back as his smile broadened. A different song drifted in through the window.

Mallaji left as Sunil's colleagues trickled into the office, clearing their throats and attending to their rituals—opening drawers, arranging receipt and ink pads, arranging stamps. The click-clack of Mallaji's numerous rings still echoed in Sunil's corner. Citizens seeking service left him unmolested for the entire morning. Sunil filed away Mallaji's documents and wondered about Thapa. He hadn't heard from Arjel in a while. What was Arjel up to, with his talk about politicians and source-force? Sunil cringed at the thought of having the plot of land taken away from him. He opened the file and studied the figures written in a messy hand in red ink. The telephone rang.

'The unthinkable has happened, babu!' Bhauju cried at the other end. 'Why are they coming after us now? Why now? Everybody is doing it. Everybody gets into the service to do it.' Bhauju ranted a good five minutes before she came to the point. 'They took away your dai, Sunil babu. Early in morning. He hadn't even finished his puja. I said, "At least let him finish his puja." But these heartless godless monsters. Why would they listen? They took him away. You have to come. You have to save your brother, babu! You have to come!'

Sunil let out a long sigh as he hung up. His colleagues asked him what the matter was. Sunil chuckled and said, 'Nothing.' He waited until one o'clock to ask his section officer for permission to visit Bhauju. 'There is no work to be done anyway, Sunilji.' The section officer looked up from his computer screen. Reflected on his large glasses was the computer screen with a game of solitaire in progress.

Sunil sipped the bland tea Bhauju had brewed for him and Wagleji. Wagleji ran a law firm that wasn't doing very well. He wasn't the most competent lawyer in town. He had a moustache that deflated his mostly incoherent arguments. He was forgetful, prone to losing his train of thought mid-sentence. That was not a good trait in a lawyer and fittingly, his firm had been suffering. But Bhauju took Sunil aside to remind him that only the rich and the corrupt would hire big-brass high-class lawyers. The logic baffled Sunil, but before he could question Bhauju, she reminded him that Wagleji was a distant relative of hers. His fees could be comfortably delayed. And in any case, she said, everyone knows how cases are won in certain courts with certain judges.

'Tell me, Wagleji, how was he to know those were stolen vehicles? How would an honest man like him tell crooks by their faces? Nobody comes with their dishonesty written in black ink on their foreheads. Do motor-gadis have mouths to say I am stolen property, I am not stolen property?'

'It is not for me to tell either way, Bhauju.' Wagleji tried to steer clear. 'It is for the judge to tell. I can only argue.'

'I am also arguing only, Wagleji!' Bhauju was in a superb form. She was being creative to save her husband, like every righteous Hindu wife ought to. Sati Savitri had set too high a bar for all Hindu women. 'What did Yudisthir say when he was asked to find one bad man? Didn't he say that a man with a pure heart doesn't see the bad in anyone else? How could my husband tell that those men were thieves? Only thieves recognize other thieves.'

'This is a legal case, Bhauju.' Sunil tried to placate her. 'They don't listen to stories from the Mahabharat in courts. There are papers, laws and lawyers, dates and arguments. Wagleji knows best. Let him handle it all.'

'You'll have to tell me the details,' Wagleji politely interjected. Hari dai smiled down at them from a portrait in a gilded frame—a smart tie and a very distinguished pair of spectacles added an unreal charisma to the absentee.

On a misty February morning, an unprecedented two dozen vehicles of various models had pulled into the back lot of a customs office on the southern border. Twenty-four rapidly written registrations had entered twenty-five wrong chassis numbers. Hari dai's signature had endorsed them all. Sunil remembered Mallaji's wisdom. Of course, all hands make mistakes when copying numbers. Just a slip of the hand, a lapse of mind; an added number here, a strange figure there.

With Wagleji's assistance, Bhauju started a tally of relatives, acquaintances and simply corrupt officials who could be approached. She also counted her jewellery, the cash in various banks, money her relatives owed, and the price the piece of land in the village would fetch, if it came to that.

Sunil looked at Bhauju and then at Hari dai's photo. He looked at the room. The furniture in the room was expensive, surely. How much did the large television set cost? The decor around him was vulgarly ambitious, extravagant beyond Hari dai's position, no matter how lucrative the customs posting had been.

The more Sunil pondered the accumulated ostentatious touch of wealth around the room, the more a mild, acceptable face of corruption suggested itself to his mind.

He couldn't afford morality in the same breath as he drew with his meagre salary. Morality, his wife's dreams and Sunil couldn't sleep in the same bed. It doesn't belong here, Sunil thought. It should be swept under this expensive carpet, and drowned by the cheap music blaring from the large television set.

Sunil hadn't prepared himself for what awaited him at home.

'Here he comes! Sunilji! Welcome to your own house!' Mallaji laughed good-naturedly and shook his ample belly. Nanu looked at his imposing moustache and giggled. Nirmala gently led Nanu to Maya didi's room.

'Mallaji!' Sunil was surprised. 'You should have come to the office.'

Nirmala returned to the room and sat on the bed. Sunil took off his shoes and put them away in a corner. The penury that pervaded his room ashamed Sunil. He felt that his hypocrisy, that he was in no need to sell his morality for a meagre sum of money, had been exposed by the patchy rug and the damp, peeling walls.

'Thirsty man must go to the well, don't they say?' Mallaji said with a zealous grin. 'You are such a big man, and I am only begging you for your favour. I should come to you. I thought, Let's go visit Sunilji at his home, make matters easier. It isn't good to be seen too often in your office—it isn't very nice for you. Gives people reason to talk behind your back.'

'What does it matter what people say? If I have no guilt in my heart, there is no blemish on my soul.'

'Now there, you said it yourself!' Mallaji slapped his thigh and jumped on his chair. 'You are a wise man after all, Sunilji. No blemish on the soul if there's no guilt in the heart. Now, let me ask you, Nirmala bahini,' Mallaji turned to Sunil's wife, 'let me ask you—is there guilt in providing for your daughter what she deserves, if it comes to you by itself? Isn't it sin to turn away Lachhimi when she comes to your doorstep?'

'I'm not saying that you don't deserve to revive your business. But I'm not the right man for this. I've never taken bribes before.'

'Ram! Ram! How you speak of it, Sunilji!' Mallaji cut in. 'So many forms of dharma there are for a man to uphold. I understand professional integrity. Do you think I don't fear my conscience when I have to wash my hands in dirty waters to put a morsel in my children's mouths? But that is the karma of men, Sunilji. We have to sometimes ask our conscience to keep a vow of silence so that we may fulfil our other duties in life. If Arjun had to kill his kinsmen to do his dharma, what great penance is it to ask your conscience to take a break once in a while? And Sunilji, trust me on this—the conscience sits much happier on a contended spirit.'

'You don't have to call it a bribe, you know,' Sunil's wife suggested.

'It isn't to say that I don't want to help you. But I don't want to dirty my hands. I won't take any money.'

'I'll find a way of helping myself. You are wise beyond your years, Sunilji. I'm sure you understand that one hand needs another to wash itself.'

'So, what are you suggesting?' Nirmala asked.

'I'm suggesting let's have that cup of tea you said you'd give me,' Mallaji said and laughed.

Mallaji didn't stay long after he finished his tea. Nanu had wandered back into the room, so he picked the child and bounced her on his knee, making faces at her, wiggling his big moustache. Sunil drank his tea and watched the businessman play with his daughter. Mallaji made a big show of carrying the cup to the red plastic tub in the corner where Nirmala washed the dishes, and Nirmala protested, just as decorum demanded. They amused Sunil—the man who'd insinuated his way into his home to corrupt him, and the wife who'd opened the gates to make the defeat possible.

That night was a difficult one. Nirmala cooked an elaborate meal. Her bright face lit up the small room and delighted Nanu. Nirmala started counting the months it would take them before they could finish building the house and move in. Sunil picked an old *Garima* magazine and reread a short story his friend Amod had published in it.

Then she counted how much more they would have to pay as rent to the landlord before they had a place of their own, and the sum displeased her. 'We could buy a gas stove and a whole new set of utensils with that much money,' she said once. 'We could buy a dining table for the kitchen,' she said as she dished out the mutton curry to Sunil and Nanu, who patiently sat on a straw mat on the floor. 'We could even buy a small fridge,' she said as she put away the leftovers. 'We could buy a decent bed with thick mattress,' she said as she slipped into the bed and took away the magazine he was reading. Sunil pasted an ambivalent expression on his face and looked at the ceiling.

Sunil felt restless, annoyed at how slowly Saturday passed. Nirmala was cautious around him ever since Mallaji surprised him that day. He was also worried that Mallaji might choose to visit in the evening. As he put on his shoes, Sunil asked Nirmala if he should bring anything for the evening. She looked at him with worry in her eyes and shook her head.

He had forgotten to ask Arjel where his sick wife was confined. But he remembered that she suffered from a respiratory disease. He didn't mind it too much that he didn't know where to go—he actually found it refreshing, walking in this well of decay and death. They were the unfortunate ones, and he was fortunate to have his health, his child, his choices.

Arjel was slumped on a bench outside a female ward.

Sunil hesitated for a moment, knowing that he could choose to walk away, to severe the connection they had. What was it that they had together? It was no friendship. Yet, he felt tied to the old man and his dreams.

'Arjel sir,' Sunil said. Arjel shifted a few inches on the bench. Sunil didn't sit. 'How is she now?' he asked.

'She is eating. I twisted the son's ears while she was sleeping and made him say he would stay, not go to Korea. I'll use source-force to get him a job here, I told the mother and son.' Source-force, again. Sunil knew it must have pained Arjel to have to say that to the son, after how Dhungel's people had treated the old teacher the first time around.

Arjel's wife was sitting up in her bed, eating yellow jaulo rice. She wasn't enjoying her meal. Sunil did a namaste, and she nodded. 'Sunil babu, the one who wants to buy that land,' Arjel said as he sat on the edge of her bed.

'You should, Sunil babu,' Arjel's wife said. 'You are young, you have a government job. Old people like us; we should go back to our own village to die.'

'Don't say that,' Arjel said to his wife, 'don't say such things.' Sunil saw the tenderness between them. He smiled, said she should think of good things, and eat more. Arjel's wife smiled back and nodded. She wasn't old—no more than Bhauju's age, Sunil thought—but she had had a hard life, no doubt.

In the corridor outside, Arjel sat on the bench. 'I don't like it inside. Too much talk of death. It tires me out,' he said. Sunil sat by Arjel's side. He wanted to ask Arjel for advice. About Hari dai's predicament, about Mallaji, about Nirmala's suddenly unchecked ambitions. But what would he say? How would be broach the subject without appearing selfish and petty?

Arjel pointed to a young man hurrying towards them. He carried a clear plastic folder filled with documents. 'The son,' Arjel said.

'How is she now?' the young man asked.

'She is eating,' Sunil volunteered.

'Better now, better,' Arjel said. 'In a day or two she can go home.' The young man scrutinized Sunil.

'This is Sunil babu. He also wants to buy the land,' Arjel said. Sunil saw the young man's face betray a shade of bitterness before politely nodding. Sunil returned his greeting.

On Sunday, Sunil stood in line to have his name registered and his pockets emptied. He had expected the security checks to be stricter than they were, but the guards were surprisingly polite and relaxed. 'Please go ahead,' he was told, and so he went ahead. The walls were damp and cold. He couldn't shake off the feeling that he had walked through the barred corridor before, although he knew he had never been in this part of the city, let alone the jail.

Hari dai was still reading the morning newspapers. The

guard on duty tapped on the bars. Hari dai looked up and grinned at Sunil. The guard handed Hari dai a packet of cigarettes and asked for a cigarette for himself. Sunil noticed the casual nature of their interaction. He was mildly disappointed. One had to break rules to be made to sit under guard, behind bars. How could Hari dai grin at him from behind the bar, helping the guard light his cigarette, as if his only mistake had been that of getting caught?

Sunil couldn't help but grin back because Hari dai looked like a boy enjoying the punishment because he had enjoyed the crime even more. There was a wild and satisfied gleam in his eyes—something Sunil knew from a long, long time ago, when Hari dai had indeed been a happy-go-lucky devil in the village, pulling pranks and picking fights. Sunil had imagined that Hari dai would never regain that light after marrying and joining his government job.

'What happened, dai?' asked Sunil.

'You know what happened,' Hari dai said in a warm voice. 'Saap!' he called out to the guard who had brought him the packet of cigarettes. 'Is there a chair for my younger brother here? He is with the Ministry, and he is very helpful.'

'You must have been very helpful yourself, Hari sir!' the guard said. They all laughed.

'Bhauju is doing everything that can be done, Hari dai. We have found a lawyer and Bhauju is trying to get in touch with the judge's wife. Wagleji was saying that something can be done from inside the department itself.'

'Did you say Wagle?' Hari dai asked. 'That man is an imbecile. He is no good.'

'Bhauju insisted on him. You can take a suspension of a year and then accept an appointment for a year or so in a remote customs office somewhere in the north. You know how those customs offices are. Bhauju says you can easily get away by taking an unpaid leave.'

'Forget unpaid leave. I don't care what happens with this case. I hope it takes as long as it takes to resolve.'

'What are you saying, Hari dai?' Sunil asked in amazement. The guard, who was listening to their conversation, giggled.

'How bad can this be, Sunil?' Hari dai surveyed his cell. 'The job is not pleasant and the wife is a torture to live with. I have absolutely no love for that woman. She cooks my food, she washes my clothes and she is the mother of my children, but that is it. I never thought of her as anything more than my wife. I did not choose to marry her—Father chose her for me. And I consented. Why would I not? And since the day I married her she has pushed me, every day, to make more money, buy more jewellery, build a bigger house, send my children to more expensive schools than her sister's children go to. I have long ceased being her husband—I am only a machine that makes money for her. And I did sign those twenty-four false registrations. All for money. All for money that she wanted me to make for her. She can chew on all that cash if it gives satisfaction. I hope it gives her indigestion.'

Sunil searched for words to counter Hari dai's rant. 'You know how wives can be.'

'Don't take it to mean that I didn't take pleasure in doing what I did. I liked making money, too, but my greed had its limits. Her greed has no shame and no limits. If I had done all that she asked of me, I would have made enough money to never have to come to this cell. It is necessary, Sunil, to know when to be greedy and when to stop. It is more necessary to know when one has to be greedy.'

Sunil had nothing to say. He had never had a very close relationship with Hari dai—they were brothers, their relationship had been established by blood. There was no need to fortify that bond. They rarely communicated, and they never shared personal opinions or concerns. This new side of Hari dai was a revelation to Sunil.

'How is that plot of land coming through?'

'You know how it is.'

Hari dai thought for a while. 'You will never get anywhere without learning the truth about the world.' Hari dai grabbed Sunil's hand and exhaled a large lungful of smoke before continuing. 'The truth about the world is that it is only a crime to be caught. It is not a crime to break rules. What do they teach your little girl in school? That we have to be truthful and ambitious. Show me one man who has been happy without breaking a few rules, without feeding on the misery of a few others. If you can flaunt your success, your immoral acts become inconsequential.'

'Are you comfortable here?' Sunil asked Hari dai when it was time to leave.

'Comfort is a relative thing.' Hari dai was obviously inventing maxims for himself, preparing for whatever the outcome of the case. 'I don't mind it a bit here. I have Saap here for a friend, and I get to read the day's newspapers after everyone is through. That is all the business I need to keep myself occupied. Tell your Bhauju I am very comfortable, and that I am not missing her cooking or the comfort of my bed.'

Just as Sunil left the police station he heard loud laughter from Hari dai's cell. The guard giggled beside him. A few drunken men had sobered up overnight and embarrassedly looked at their toes as the inspector melted them with his furious gaze.

Outside the prison gate, the sun was out, brilliant and crisp; there wasn't a single cloud in the sky.

That night, Nanu slept peacefully in her corner. Nirmala placed her hand on Sunil's chest. She bit his earlobe. Sunil turned away even though he felt his passion awake. It had been an interesting day. They hadn't talked about his visit to the jail. She did not yet know what Hari dai thought of his sojourn as a guest of the state. If she knew how comfortable Hari dai seemed with his situation, Sunil wondered if Nirmala would be even more demanding about the possibility of cutting a deal with Mallaji. The other day, as Mallaji drank tea, Nirmala had surprised Sunil with her audacity and scheming—Mallaji had agreed with most of what she proposed, and kept praising her, calling her his sworn sister. Sunil had sat mum through their agitated planning.

As he dressed for office the next morning, Sunil felt strangely naked, inadequate. He asked Nirmala to let the dirty dishes be for the moment and come sit by him, took her hands in his, and spoke softly. Nirmala seemed frightened by his very serious demeanour, his deliberate voice. But as the thrust of the conversation became clearer, she started giggling. Sunil found it inappropriate for the situation, but this, too, was his dharma—to make his wife laugh with joy, no matter where the joy was borrowed or thieved from.

But instead of heading to the Ministry, Sunil found himself hopping off the microbus at the Teaching Hospital stop. Arjel's son was sitting on the bench outside his mother's ward. 'Where is Arjel sir?' Sunil asked.

Arjel's son walked into the ward. His mother was bent double on the bed, rocking to and fro, crying quietly into hospital pillows. A teary-eyed nurse sat by her side. 'Ama,' the nurse said, 'Ama, who could have said this would happen? At least he went peacefully. Ama, take comfort in that.'

Sunil stepped out and sat on the bench where Arjel used to sit. How did this happen? Why today? Why had Sunil felt the urge to visit Arjel in the first place? Arjel's son sniffled, crossed his arms and stared at Sunil.

'You put the idea into his head,' Arjel's son said. 'He talked about how he was going to buy the land with you, build a house together. He kept talking about the house all the time, kept telling Mother we'd live here now.'

Sunil gaped at Arjel's son. He thought the young man's words were full of hate, although he had said nothing hateful yet.

'I could have gone to Korea. Sent back money to take care of them. But he wanted to buy that land, build the house.'

Sunil stood and stared at the spot on the bench that he has just vacated. He shut out from his head what Arjel's son was saying and, unable to shed tears for Arjel, he walked away.

His colleagues were already seated at their tables when he reached the Ministry. Citizens lined up before each bureaucrat. Sunil barely had time to arrange his stamps before citizens swarmed his desk. Between signing and stamping, he looked up: Mallaji was fourth in line, his papers at the ready. When Mallaji's turn came, Sunil opened the drawer where he kept his red pen.

Over the next months, Sunil agreed to pay Mallaji a very low interest on the loan he took from the hotel. Surely there could be no law against that. And which hand doesn't slip once in a while? Which mind doesn't lapse once in a while? In any case, the under-secretary who had written the original figures in red ink had terrible handwriting too.

Hari dai's house also buzzed with activity. Nirmala

wanted to pitch in and help Bhauju, but Sunil discouraged it. Bhauju made one phone call after another, employing the four principles of saam, daam, danda and bhed to get her way: pleading and reasoning, bribing, threatening and poisoning the ears of rivals. Her brothers were employed full-time to seek possible allies in the court. The judge's sister frequented Hari dai's home and Bhauju prepared elaborate teas. But she soon lost her energy and settled into calmness as the date for the court proceedings approached.

The day arrived. Hari dai played with Nanu. Bhauju admired the front door, but Nirmala said there was another door that she had liked more—one with Shiva and Parvati carved on it. It was much too expensive, and Sunil had said, 'What good is having gods on the front door if you will already have a separate room for worshipping?'

Mallaji's wife showed Nirmala her wristwatch. She was happy that Nirmala admired it, because Mallaji planned to surprise Nirmala with a similar wristwatch as a present for the occasion. Nanu had a bicycle waiting while Sunil would have to be content with a hundred-litre refrigerator.

Mallaji had spotted his vein of gold in Nirmala. What Sunil did not know was that Mallaji had plans to assist his hotelier relatives with their water problems.

Mallaji's generous limb circled Sunil's shoulders. Mallaji wasn't half as bad as a man. Sunil had become quite fond of him and his wife. Between his full-hearted laughs and not very funny remarks at which he himself laughed far more than his audience would, Mallaji still spoke a few words of such worldly wisdom as Sunil had only recently begun to appreciate.

'Sunilji! How is business?' Mallaji asked.

'You are the one with a business, Mallaji. It isn't good for a businessman to forget he has a business to run, you know.' Sunil knew where Mallaji was going with the conversation. It was still discomfiting when Mallaji called him a businessman, but Sunil had learned to make friends with the alligator of still waters.

'Of course. You are right, Sunilji!' Mallaji saw his joke home and laughed to shake the newly paned windows. Nanu heard him laugh and giggled.

Mallaji heard her giggle and laughed some more at her. His wife fondly shook her head.

'Business must be good.' Hari dai, who had so far been listening to the women, turned to Mallaji. 'Look how happy he looks. His cheeks are juicy like a young woman's.'

Mallaji and Hari dai laughed again. Sunil turned to the house: the four walls of his dream were in place now. The windows did catch the sunlight. But in his dreams Sunil had never imagined the walls in colour. Nirmala had chosen the carpets and curtains. Above all, she had shown herself to be a very thoughtful spender, not at all like Bhauju. That pleased Sunil.

'Where is the bahun?' asked Hari dai.

A frail old man was led to Sunil's house by a ten-year-old. 'Grandfather cannot see,' he explained. Grandfather had no teeth but the child understood all of his commands and smartly prepared the yajna.

So this is how it is to have a home of one's own, Sunil thought. A home built on one's sweat and blood. And a good measure of dishonesty. But where would honesty shelter itself in turbulent storms and freezing cold if one did not have a house of one's own? These bricks will soak my wife's laughter, my child's prattle. When the colours on these walls fade, it will not be time corroding them—it will be my days as husband and father, the joys and sorrows, the hardship and rewards, painting the walls anew. New furniture will be broken in; sofas will have hollows into which I will sink gratefully.

A branch of bougainvillea will snake up to the roof and I will be able to point to my house from afar, from the city, from the hills, and my friends will smile and slap my back. I will be able to open my doors to friends and strangers alike, and they will know that they are in my house, that I am the owner of this house. Within these walls I will fear no one, not even providence.

'Where are you lost, Sunilji?' Mallaji's mammoth limb landed on Sunil's shoulders again. 'Grandfather is calling for the yajaman.'

Nanu wanted to sit on Sunil's lap as he headed to the yajna fire but Nirmala held her back. 'Let her come,' Sunil said. 'It is her home, after all.' After an hour of chants and throwing ghee-soaked barley into the fire, Nirmala broke a fresh coconut on the threshold of the house. Bhauju cried on the shoulder of Mallaji's wife as Nirmala ceremoniously entered the house.

The house is still there, with a storey added since it was built. A gentle, acceptable mixture of colours adorns its façade. When Nirmala's mother visited the new house, she built a mound for a tulsi plant by the gate. Bhauju brought a cutting of bougainvillea. The holy tulsi plant is taking roots into the rich, dark Kathmandu soil while a colourful spray of bougainvillea rises ambitiously to the skies.

THE FACE OF
CAROLYNN FLINT

I have learned my lessons now, but there was a time when I thought of myself as a student of life, an aspiring artist who would learn from observation alone and later reproduce the minutiae of everyday to feed his work; in fiction, painting and cinema. These were my ambitions—I suppose I should say they still remain my ambitions, I haven't given up yet. I was keen on note-taking, which meant I always chose dark corners in a pub or restaurant, or sat apart from a crowd waiting for the bus.

In Walla Walla of Washington state in the U.S., where I spent four years alternately feeling gratefully ensconced in the warm camaraderie of my friends and feeling intensely, incurably alone, I patronized the Mill Creek Brew-Pub. On the couple of occasions when I got my heart broken I talked to the barkeep, Rebecca, the father of whose three children was deployed to Iraq. We made an unenviable pair of whiners, saying the silliest things about the other sex to make each other laugh. If ever I came close to being a regular at any establishment, it was there. I'd go in feeling down and I'd leave somewhat happy after a pint or two. I always felt welcome there, even on days when I felt alienated, atomized, so far from Nepal, separated from the friends and everything familiar I had grown up with.

I left Walla Walla on a bus because I had an interview scheduled in Palo Alto for a week after graduation. My closest friends—from my high school years in Kathmandu and from Whitman—were in the Bay Area: Basu in Santa Rosa, Tuan and Huyen in San Mateo, and Anu in Mountain View. Mithun was starting his PhD at Stanford. The job seemed promising in the heady years before the Great Recession. There's money on the floor, people in the Silicon Valley said, you just have to bend over to pick it. I got the job. It made the parents happy, and some close friends at college who had wondered what I'd make of myself seemed relieved.

But I wasn't one for bending over so much, I realized, so I quit the job and started looking for menial work. An old man at an ice cream parlour grabbed my palms, kneaded them, and told me I lacked the temperament for running his joint. So after blundering through an undergraduate education, I made an itinerant fool's journey through a job or two and ended up in Santa Rosa, a small town north of San Francisco. I arrived at Basu's door a destitute but in high spirits, flipping in the air the one-quarter coin that was all of my monetary worth. He showed me The Russian

River Brewery on 4th Street. It was a mostly crowded place with impressive casks of new beer fermenting right behind the bar. They were creative with the names they gave their brews: Perdition, Pliny the Elder, Damnation. A brew that was always on the menu but never on tap was called Procrastination. Wood was the first impression the place gave—everything was finished in varnished wood. They had live music few days a week. It was a popular place, and those who liked it liked drinking beer. I doubt it was much of a place to meet other people, but it was popular enough and people came to unwind after a day's work.

If I am not mistaken, it was in the month of September that I met Carolynn there. It was the middle of the day; I had just got off the Number 80 bus returning from San Rafael where I worked as a copy-writer at an Internet marketing firm. The afternoon was warm, and I had some money. A woman smiled at me from across the long bar and I smiled back. I was used to being smiled at by older women, and it wasn't difficult to tell that she was older than she let on. She moved closer, sat next to me and said she wanted to buy me another beer. I had work to finish after returning home, but a free beer sounded better. Writing could always wait while life happened. Habit takes slaves.

At first sight, she didn't have a plain face. She seemed to catch all the lights, and whichever way she turned, she still looked decent, something rare among the patrons of Russian River. She must get incrementally more attractive with every subsequent pint, I thought. When she inched closer, I realized there was something of a heavy hand of the sculptor about her visage, something calculated. Her hair couldn't be its natural colour—that would be too much to ask for. Every woman in California gets a nose job or a boob job, so I thought, She isn't any more out of the ordinary than the next woman in the street. I didn't know what she looked like before she got it fixed, whatever it was that she had got fixed, so who was I to judge? I think she misunderstood my curiosity, the way I leaned in to check if she was wearing contacts or her eyes were really the colour they were, because she looked down with thickly mascaraed eyes, looked away for a beat and a half and looked back again. I have always found that fascinating, the dance of eyes that women have. I smiled at her and raised my beer, looking at her over the rim.

Before I talk about Carolynn, I should talk about Heather. It is a bit of a digression, but there are common elements in both their stories and I will return to Carolynn in due course. In any case, if Carolynn's eyes hadn't reminded me of Heather's, I wouldn't have settled into the sort of familiarity that makes a person easy game. Heather is younger than me by almost three years. When I saw her for the first time, the evening before my first day at Whitman College, she had thick brown hair that reached her waist, a mouth full of teeth that were perfectly straight, and a slow, mournful walk. We were in a house off-campus, to drink beer and meet new people, and without deliberate design, the handful of people gathered there were all outsiders, from far-flung corners: Lea from Croatia and wearing a bindi from Pune; Tuan from Vietnam by the way of Seattle; Yuan Ming from Taiwan, who'd put up the portrait of Chiang Kai-shek in the kitchen downstairs; Shiv Karan from Kolkata; and me, from Kathmandu. And there was Heather, from a boat anchored off the shore of Juno, Alaska. She was eighteen, taller than me by half an inch, and she always smelled good. Over the year, regardless of whether or not she had a boyfriend at the time, I tried to persuade her to get into a relationship with me. I was somewhat relentless, if there are degrees of it. I wanted to talk her into it, reason it with her. After we'd been close friends for two years, she said that though she did love me, she just didn't trust me as a potential boyfriend. She astonished me with diagnosis. 'I know you're the kind that cheats. I am scared to fall in love with you because I know it won't end well. For either of us.' She had a way of pausing between her sentences and hitting me when I didn't expect it. The second sentence usually came with a sudden flick of the head, her eyes squinting and her hair flipping like a mare's tail, her face opening to catch more light in which I was to see how strongly she believed in what she said.

Heather had beautiful eyes. I always thought the colour of her eyes was that of water off the coast of Alaska, somewhere near Juno, where she grew up on a fourteen-foot fishing boat, waking up to coats and hats warmed in the oven by her mother. Her eyes changed colour constantly: sometimes the paleness of a late summer sky and sometimes the blue-green of bits of glass found on the beach but, nevertheless, something glassy and oceanic about them remained. Later, when we were together, I would wake up in the night and see her shoulder lit by the moon and the light of the street outside. I'd kiss it every time: a sort of mindless romantic gesture I surprised myself with. She'd turn over sometimes and open her eyes, still asleep, her lips curled. When we finally broke up, the hardest thing was to forget how her eyes looked in the night.

Heather had understood something essential about me, a truth about my nature upon which everything else is founded. And she had showed it to me in her contradictory manner: it was plain to her that I was incapable of telling the truth to those I loved, and that my eyes were ravenously, prodigiously of the wandering sort; that, despite every reason I had given her before our relationship started, I was hollow and with nothing to offer by way of genuine love. I resorted to cheap sentimentality or cold reason as one or the other suited me best. All of this Heather saw and understood, but she loved me despite everything; in the irrational, unsentimental way that only she could.

Once, when a man should just cuddle his woman and grunt in agreement, stroking her arm and kissing her hair and neck, I asked, 'What do you hate the most about me?'

She turned and kissed me lightly on the lips. 'I hate it when you make me wait,' she said. 'I hate it when you come to me drunk in the middle of the night.' But we never fought. Not once. Until that day when I asked her what she expected from me. That night we slept on opposite sides of the bed, although, through the sleepless night our feet or hands touched, never breaking contact through the night. Sometimes the thread that joins two hearts is no more than a few square inches of skin in conversation.

Carolynn was still smiling at me, swirling the beer in her glass. Carolynn Flint, born in Cloverdale, or some other small town in Oregon, I can't remember. Four years of waiting tables in San Francisco got her nowhere. Tired of that, she trained to be a real estate agent, and now she was successful, with a staff of four working for her eight, nine houses listed in the market. She had an office on B Street, a quaint little cottage with weathered shingles and stained-glass windows, disparate but elegantly put together. She had been married twice, amicably divorced once, and now she was independent. We talked for a bit.

Her eyes responded to the answers I gave about myself. She asked me if I wanted to see her office. 'But it is only two o'clock,' I said. It felt a bit foolish. She laughed the peal of a glamorous, confident woman. With one hand she touched my knee and with the other she ran a finger over my wrist.

On the wall of her office, behind her desk, was a row of framed photographs. It was as if she had modelled for an amateur painting class and collected the class assignments afterwards. There was a vase with white flowers on the uncluttered desk, a combination printer-scanner-fax machine, a potted plant in the corner closest to a large window, three chairs of a set, and a framed picture of a lake surrounded by high mountains. It was a fairly regular office space.

She smiled at me, her head cocked to a side as she gauged me. I looked at the pictures again, starting with her at the very end of the row of photos, scrutinizing the line of faces. It was the same person in each picture: Carolynn, of course. But in each picture her face was different. Hair colour and style changed significantly between pictures, but the shape of the face remained the same. The nose changed a little, the arch of the eyebrows traced different curves, the cheekbones sidled, and a cleft chin erupted in the line-up to abruptly disappear again. It was like watching the frames of a movie-reel melting a little as each passed the lamp, or, it was like watching a lump of clay after each pass between a careful pair of hands. I looked at Carolynn, who laughed with perfect teeth and nose all bunched up, ringlets of hair falling from the temples.

'Are these your pictures?' I asked.

'Um. What do you think?'

'It is all you,' I said, involuntarily taking a step closer to her. She reacted with her body, like a dancer or a chorus responding to a beat, skipping on her feet. The office was surprisingly empty for the time of the day. Sunlight reflecting off a patch of grey carpet lit her chins and eyes; her breasts cast a shadow above them, accentuating the orbs, drawing my eyes to them. I was close enough to her that I smelled her perfume more than the beer on her breath.

There was something vaguely erotic about being stared at by five women, each remarkably alike yet different, and having the carnal corpus, flesh and heaving breath, in warm proximity, putting me in the centre of a ring of fixed attention. Or, perhaps it was the beer and the cool white of reflected sunlight and a California afternoon, but something inside me was stirred awake; suddenly every extension of my body, each sense and more, became a surveyor of the distance between us.

I met Carolynn again in the evening after sleeping off the buzz of the afternoon's beer. She did something unusual when I walked into the place: she got off the stool and showed herself off, did a little twirl and even said 'ta-da!' She must have been checking the door, or even the street outside. Her face lit up from within, which made me very happy, giddy even. I kissed her cheek and she hugged me. I had to tell her to let me breathe, then she giggled and let go.

She lived in a house that looked almost like her office: the same carpet, the same kinds of plants in pots in corners around the room, the same row of photographs. There wasn't a single picture of another person. I had to use the bathroom, so I went, and when I came back, I leaned in and kissed her. She locked her fingers in my hair. Good thing I had not gone entirely bald at the back of my head yet, or it would have been embarrassing; she could have pulled out tufts of my very fine, thinning hair, and where would that have taken us?

I saw later that night that no knife had touched her below the neck. She had taken care of herself very well—none of the stringy sinews of a fitness fiend, nor the pockets of comforting blubber that manages to stick to women her age. She was even youthful neck down, but in the same cured way as meat: the flesh yielded to the touch, softened and juiced. The pair of depressions just above the buttocks were deep, and the back was a bronze expanse of fine down; the breasts quirky, each with its own particular stare. When she covered herself in play, ruby-red nails added a blast of colour to the night.

I was looking at the ceiling and counting tiles, not really thinking anything, but letting the mind wander when it occurred to me that I might not see Carolynn again. All of this—the attraction of an older woman, the colour of her nails, the pictures on the wall—all seemed fine as a part of something that wasn't meant to last. I had never seen her before, and it seemed natural, even necessary, that it all end there, that night. I turned towards her and she also turned, pushing a knee between my knees, hand reaching behind the waist, the dampness of recent exertion colliding, coalescing.

'How come I never saw you before?' I asked. I had really meant to ask if I'd be seeing her again. I didn't want to give the false impression that I particularly wanted to see her again. It was satisfying to not be tied to anyone, not even casually. I wasn't looking for companionship during those days. The job I had wasn't working out so well, and I needed desperately to get back to writing, even if only for the sake of keeping my sanity.

'I've seen you before,' she said, 'walking in your turquoise crocs.' I guess she had seen me before, if she'd seen me in my turquoise crocs. 'I've seen you walking to the Junior College, I've seen you at the farmers' market. I even saw you on Fourth of July. You were the one who wasn't dancing, but your friends were.'

I could only laugh. And it occurred to me that it is very rarely that we need to justify a laugh, even a sudden, clipped laugh: it is a vanquisher of so many avatars of awkwardness, a statement of reassurance, sometimes the purest, most solid response to helplessness.

Heather didn't do that. Instead of letting the tension dissipate with a laugh, even a forced one, she crinkled her forehead and pursed her mouth. Except once. She had a talent for that: the singular twist with which she changed like a face on a Rubik's Cube, irreversibly different, indecipherable with the tools functional until that moment.

That was how we got into a relationship: she left a note under my door instead of calling me or writing it in an email, for me to find during the lunch break. She had ugly penmanship.

'I love you,' it said, 'but you scare me. It scares me to think what you could do to me. I don't like the idea that you would hurt me more than I have been hurt before. I know you would love me equally,' the note said, 'but somehow, I still can't trust you.' I was not a monster when I was in college, and she tended to exaggerate the worst qualities of me, but I would've warned my women friends if one of them were to choose a guy like me. By the time I received this note, I had given up on trying to talk Heather into going out with me. Then, out of nowhere, she told me that she loved me. It was the third week into our relationship: I still considered it the trial phase; but she couldn't just be saying that she loved me as a friend. 'That's okay,' was my first response. She stopped breathing. I could sense that much in the dark. I apologized and said, 'I meant to ask you if you just love me or if you are in love with me.' It wasn't a good beginning to a relationship in which we would later come to make absurd promises. Heather had wanted to name our eventual, inevitable, son after a cat she'd had as a child, and after just a few minutes of protest, I had agreed to it.

Our son would have been named Alistair, after a dead cat. No wonder the relationship didn't last. Of course, my being myself didn't help much, but I also blame Heather.

She should have not been so obstinate about her belief that I could never change. She should have asked me to change, for her sake, for the sake of the future we were supposed to share. She didn't, so I didn't, and here I was now, in Santa Rosa, at least three thousand miles away from Heather, laughing in response to being found out by Carolynn.

Carolynn had seen me before, perhaps she saw me share a turkey leg with Basu at the Fourth of July fair. Perhaps she saw me digging my teeth with a finger to dislodge a string of turkey tendon.

'You've been eyeing me then, haven't you?' I asked.

It was her turn to laugh. 'What could I do? You were there, always with an intense look. And your crocs, everywhere you went.' Perhaps, through the scowl on my face and the permanence of striking footwear I had been signalling something which she caught. She buried her face into my chest and breathed with an open mouth. I lifted the sheets, threw it to the floor, reached over her and switched on the reading lamp. She gave a yelp, a coquettish laugh which came from the womb.

I sat at the foot of the bed and looked at her. She took her hands behind her head and stretched. A toe touched my belly and danced up to the shoulder. When our faces were close, eyes locking in the shadow of our arms, she didn't look like anyone in the pictures on the wall. Close enough that I could contemplate her nostrils and the individual hair of her brows: from that close, Carolynn was anywoman, essential, made real only because I admired her in that hour. She had no shape beyond that which pasted on the screen of my mind, and it was a fuller picture than the eye could see because it was written by the whole body and a longing that stretched years into the past, when the sunshine of her youth must have been differently languorous, differently warm. Such thoughts came to me.

'I wonder what you looked like a year ago,' I said. 'I wonder how you looked when you were nineteen. I want to see you naked at nineteen.'

'I was ugly then,' she said. 'You might have liked me naked, but you wouldn't have wanted to see me the next day. Were you like that as a boy?'

'I'm sure you were beautiful,' I said. It was late in the night and I was drowsy, but I was aware that I had said something clumsy, something that could make her suspicious of any affection I show her. I was in her bed. I wanted to avoid unpleasantness, and I was prepared to tell lies until morning. The nakedness of another body next to yours affects the intellect; this is no secret. Wars have been fought and cities razed over it. I wanted to fall asleep without offending Carolynn, so I asked her about the real estate market.

We exchanged phone numbers in the morning; she had made pancakes and bacon and put them in the oven, and she brought me coffee before leaving. 'Aren't you afraid I'll steal your stuff?' I called after her as she hurried out. She turned and gave me a thousand-watt smile and said, 'I'm taking all of my stuff with me.' Then Carolynn pressed her small breasts together with her arms and shook them and blew air kisses.

All of this—the familiarity that developed overnight, the easy lethargy of sleeping in a strange bed, being stared at by five similar women and enjoying the attention, looking forward to the next meeting—put me in a frame of mind where I let caution become dull. It felt like I had been sitting in a favourite chair, reading something full of metaphysical fantasies. The air through the window became warmer as the morning ripened and it lulled the mind, and although a part of me thought to move to another, cooler place, the warm air enticed, and the mind gave into the temptation and baked. It was a slow, sinking feeling, like standing on a sand bog and wiggling the toes to sink, ever so slowly, to the toes, mid-shins, knees, until staying rooted becomes second nature.

Now that I look back at it, all of it seems strange: how, after almost a year of going without intimacy, I had allowed myself to become familiar with a woman overnight; and I don't just mean physically, but in every way. It made me light-headed. I read and wrote a bit through the day, did laundry and waited. The evening light seeping into the trees along the streets seemed theatrically pointed at the night to come. It felt just right to finish a couple of beers before Carolynn met me at the brew pub, so I got there an hour early. I had my notebook with me, into which I variously doodled and wrote ideas to be developed into short stories, perhaps out of a guilt that I had failed to apply myself to what I thought of as my calling: writing.

I sat at the bar, scribbling story ideas into my notebook, waiting for Carolynn. An Ethiopian man, I forget his name now, sat next to me. We had talked before, about politics, most likely, and now he described a basketball game he'd seen on TV. The place was getting noisier. A woman outside knocked on the window and waved. It was somebody's birthday, a crowd of twenty-somethings started to sing, so I raised my glass at the end of the cheer. I swivelled on the stool to check if Carolynn had come in through the back door, but she was nowhere to be seen.

I felt a tap on my shoulder, but I paid no attention, thinking perhaps someone just wanted me to scoot closer to the bar to make room for them to walk to the restrooms. I turned when I felt a hand grab my arm. It was the woman who'd waved from outside. 'Excuse me,' I said, 'do I know you?' She looked at me, a little frustrated, a little disappointed, gave me a wan smile and made her way to the back of the pub, to the women's room. Carolynn was still not in. Could she be one of Carolynn's friends, I thought, does she think I should know her? Carolynn hadn't introduced me to anybody. Her face seemed familiar, but that is true about most faces if familiarity is what I scan them for in the first place. It is the same few bricks: nose, a pair of eyes, lips of varying thickness and mouth stretched far or little, offset by ears funny or not; it is the same few things that distinguish between the ones we love and the ones we can let die with no more than cheap pity thrown their way.

The woman returned and stood by me. 'It's me,' she whispered. The beer I had just sipped went straight through my nose. She sounded freakishly like Carolynn. 'It's me,' she said, her hand sliding down my arm to find the palm. 'It's me, Carolynn. It's me.' She rubbed my palm and her nose became damp. I stood, one hand on the bar, the other wiping on my shirt to get rid of the condensation from the beer glass.

'I don't understand. Is this a joke? Do you know Carolynn?'

'I am she,' she said. 'I know what you're thinking. You're thinking I don't look like Carolynn, and right now, I don't look like me, I know I don't, but I swear I am Carolynn.'

'I don't understand,' I kept saying. Even in that confusion something repeatedly tugged at my eyeballs, so that my gaze flicked to the glass of beer every four seconds or so.

I finally grabbed it and finished it in a single gulp, shaking my head, staring at her out of the corner of my eyes. I must have looked like a frightened animal. She was still rubbing my palm with both hands. I couldn't make any sense of this. Was this an erotic interrogation put together by Carolynn? What had I signed up for? Before I knew anything, I was in the street, walking absentmindedly to whichever direction she pulled me. In a minute or so, I started considering two possibilities: that this woman was indeed Carolynn, and whether the fault lay in my psyche or in her make, my senses or the fabrication of her face, I was holding hands with the same woman with whom I'd had a wonderful time; or, that this wasn't Carolynn but a friend of hers, who would make the evening even more interesting than what I had bargained for.

The more we walked, the more I became convinced it was Carolynn walking by my side. When we stopped at an intersection, for instance, when we were waiting for the light to change into a walk-sign, even though I was looking the other way, my hands could read the exact sequence of grips and tugs, when she tried to pre-empt the moment when the light would change, then hesitated because it took longer than she thought. She stood with one toe raised, foot half an inch off the ground, head searching left and right to make sure all cars had stopped, and I knew, even though I wasn't looking at her, that it was the same person who had hesitated and lifted a toe yesterday at the same intersection. I pulled her closer and put my arm around her waist. She put her arm around my waist. We matched strides and crossed the street. She didn't smile anymore; serenity enveloped her face.

We got under the sheets and sat up, still dressed, arms around each other. Cars in the street lit the room with beams that swerved in an arc; it felt like we were fugitives in a terrifying story, hiding in a corner all of our own, convinced that we'd be misunderstood by everybody who searched for

us with lit torches. Carolynn barely spoke while I talked
about this and that, trying to parry the thrust of this strange
and melancholy turn of events. Yet, even after twenty
minutes of sitting together like that, I had a feeling that I
stood on thin glass, the world under my feet lit up and
extravagantly mysterious. Then Carolynn moved her feet
and pulled her hand from behind my back, leaned into me
and made herself comfortable. She grabbed an edge of the
sheet and twisted it between her thumbs, alternately
stretching it taut and folding it.

'I wanted the boys to like me, you know, in high school.
But I was never as good-looking as some of my friends.
They were the good-looking ones, and I was the girl they
kept around. There was this girl named Gina. I guess she
was the closest friend I've ever had, but she wasn't my best
friend or anything. It was always the catty, shallow kind of
friendship. I guess we needed each other, because she was
really popular but nobody could stand her, you know,
nobody wanted to be her friend in bad times. She had a
pretty face, so people wanted to be around her, but she was
a cold, cold bitch. Nobody wanted to listen to her, because
she never had anything nice to say.' Carolynn looked into a
corner in the ceiling. There must have been a hole there, a
portal through which she could look back into the past.
She told a story well, so I listened, wanting the mystery to
unfurl.

American high schools, especially the ones in
impoverished small towns, seem full of girls desperate to

make it big, always measuring themselves against what they see on TV or in magazines at the check-out line in the local grocery store: pictures of women their age, living in bodies they want, sleeping with men they'd like to sleep with. I remember a girl in Walla Walla who went to Hawaii straight after graduating from high school because she wanted to become a bikini model. She came back after two years, tanned brown and softened, carrying bags under her eyes, no longer wanting to be a model. Then she got pregnant and started working at a bar. Carolynn must have fallen in with a similar crowd.

She moved with her hot young friends from Cloverdale to make it in the big city of San Francisco. Over the next few months, she saw how prettier waitresses made more in tips, how they got better dates who took them to fancier restaurants. Her friends could name more vintages of wines than she could. Gina even started going on week-long vacations with her various boyfriends who adored her. Life wasn't easy in the big city; there were too many girls like Carolynn auditioning for the same gigs, trying to get the same waiting jobs, trying to rent the same cheap houses. She saw an advertisement in the *Bohemian* for a cosmetic surgeon, a Jewish woman who had outlined the cost-benefit analysis of various procedures: a nose job, a boob job, lifting the eyes, injecting fat into the lips to make them fuller, laser hair-removal, cheek implants, chin implants, liposuction, removing moles and warts, aligning the teeth— which, although the procedure didn't fall under the plastic surgeon's purvey, was nonetheless pertinent to the list.

Carolynn tore out the page, folded it neatly, and kept it with her person. She started taking it out when she was in the bus or sitting in a park. She felt two things grow simultaneously: her savings, and the balloon of possibilities promised by the list in her purse. She had a picture of her face enlarged and made a dozen copies of it, and on each picture she traced the outlines of what she wanted changed: make the eyes larger, remove the hair under her temples and the fuzz under her chin, peel her neck to make it look less like that of a freshly plucked chicken, hide the veins exploding on her cheeks, raise the cheekbones, sculpt the fat away just under the cheekbones, give the tip of the nose a better definition. She'd take a fashion magazine and search it for a face that best approximated the shape of her face, cut it out and put it in a zip-lock bag.

'I was waiting for my savings to get to double the amount I needed before I could get the procedures done. I took two jobs, moved away from the girls and lived with an old gay guy who needed someone to take care of the place and make him dinner twice a week. He was really nice. I'd bring leftovers from whatever restaurant I happened to be working in and put it in the fridge. Sometimes he'd eat them and leave me a five-dollar bill. I think I made a couple of hundred bucks from him just that way. Sometimes the fridge would be full of leftovers and I'd forget about them. He'd check every box to see if anything had gone bad, and he'd throw out the stuff that wasn't good to eat anymore. He was really nice. He is dead now.

'Anyway, when I had saved enough, I went to the doctor I'd read about. She was just gorgeous, and to look at her, you couldn't tell if she'd had anything done, you know? She still had that big Jewish nose, you know, but she said she wasn't born with it. She said she didn't want a woman to change to look like someone else, like J Lo or whatever, but to look like the woman she felt she was like in the inside. Like, she'd had a nose job done on her, but not to look less Jewish, because she felt like a beautiful Jewish woman and wanted to look like one. She took one look at me and she knew exactly what I needed.

'I've never felt that in my life. It was like meeting my maker. Pardon the blasphemy, but that's what it felt like. It was like someone had a hotline to God and was revising his original design, you know, with His consultations. I knew I needed whatever she'd tell me to get done, because I knew I'd be perfect afterwards. Her name is Doctor Schwartz. Muriel Schwartz. She's really good.'

That is how Carolynn's acquaintance with the fine scalpel started. Before checking in for the procedure, she had her legal name changed, although she later changed it back after her first marriage ended.

'It's not like I got a whole new face, you know? I went home a month after the procedure, and my mother couldn't even tell what had changed. She just kept saying I looked different. She said it was probably because I'd learned new make-up tricks in San Francisco. I just laughed and said, Yeah, Mom. Wasn't like that. I'd had a nose job done and got some fatty tissue removed from under the cheekbones. I ran into a guy I used to date in high school. Dave Curry. He is a used-car salesman now. He couldn't tell what was different. Maybe they weren't, you know, sophisticated, Dave and Mom. They couldn't see what'd changed because they just weren't looking for it.'

And she had been right all along—with her theory about how prettier girls made more money. She continued living with the old gay man. Now that she had more confidence in her looks, she started coming on to older men, much older than her. There was a man, a friend of the guy she lived with. Carolynn wouldn't name her first husband, but she kept repeating how good he was. A really rich guy whose wife was cheating on him and whose daughter was in prison because of a drug habit that had gone very bad. He was a very sad old man, and Carolynn felt drawn to him. 'I saw in him a part of myself, like only he and I knew how it is to be this lonely, lost person without anybody to turn to. You know that feeling?'

It might have been the sadness that clung to the guy even when he made jokes—and it seems he was a very funny man—or it might have been the way he looked at her when he poured wine, but something clicked between them. His wife asked for a divorce, so he gave it to her—and because he knew about her affairs, she couldn't take his money, not all of it. Soon after, he asked Carolynn to marry him. They lived together in bliss for three years in a large house in Sausalito. In the second year of their marriage, his daughter

Rebecca killed herself in prison. The cloak of sadness which Carolynn had managed to lift away since their marriage abruptly fell back on him, this time around in inch-thick lead sheets of grief.

'He stopped doing everything he enjoyed, except the painting, which kept him together, I guess. He had made enough money as an angel investor along with a group of his Stanford friends, but he was never a money kind of a man. He'd take me on drives through Napa and Sonoma, and we'd stop at his friends' houses. What I miss the most about him—about us—is how he used to introduce me to his friends, some of whom had daughters my age. There was always this tiny catch in his voice when he called me his wife. You see—all of his friends knew his ex-wife, and knew why they'd gotten a divorce in the first place. So when they saw how happy I made him, how proud he was to stand in their homes, holding my hand, I think it made them happy, too.

'He tried to get me interested in things he liked, you know, wine and the economy and the politics, but I didn't care. I'd get bored and I'd ask him to drive me home. Because I liked it better at home, when it was just the two of us. He'd say things like, Bethany, you make me forget how old I am. But, although I never told him this, he made me feel old, and not in a bad way at all. In a good way. He made me feel sad and happy all at once, like I could now see how the world is a miserable place, but also how I could laugh with him. You know what he called it? He called it the small-change of joy. Like in the mornings when the sun came up over East Bay, or in how the seals barked in the night.

'He'd make me stand naked in front of a mirror. He'd stand behind me, next to me, not a stitch of cloth, nothing more than his glasses between the two of us, and he'd say, Bethany, you are beautiful. But he was even more beautiful. This man who loved me. When he said things like that, when he called me Bethany, I could only see the face that I had on before I got the procedures. I mean, I could still see myself in the mirror, but it felt as if there was a sticker or a mask of the other face stuck on the spot where my face should be. So I'd close my eyes, and he'd say, Bethany, won't you look at us. Look at us.

'One day he woke me up at five in the morning. He'd been painting all night. His breath smelled of wine, but not like he had been drinking too much. I remember everything about that morning—the bay was all mist, and the sun was rising above the hills behind Berkeley. He said, come with me, Bethany, I need you. I thought he needed me to fix him some coffee or something, toast a bagel, maybe. When he'd get into painting, he'd ask me to have a pot of coffee out for him. But he didn't. He held my hand and led me to the room he was using as a studio.'

He had been painting a portrait, a family portrait, more like, of Carolynn and himself, both naked above the waist. They were seated on a small bench, and in the painting there was a mirror in the background. There you could see their naked backs, and behind them the reflection of the window, outside which you could see the bay. It felt like an afternoon, because the bay was filled with sailboats and a large, red container ship. You could almost hear the monotone of the ship's whistle. He wanted her to look at the faces he had painted. He had painted their faces from memory, even the light was from memory, and she could see how accurate his face looked. It was a picture of his face before his daughter's death filled it with grief and tugged the corners of his mouth downward.

But there was something very wrong with her face in the picture: instead of painting Bethany, he had painted Carolynn. It wasn't the crudeness of the paint or a misplaced brushstroke, it was truth itself. Her old nose had crept into the picture, and the sharp hollow under the cheekbones which he admired so much was filled again. It looked like Bethany, of course, but it was unmistakably Carolynn. How could he know, she thought, how could he draw me like how I looked? I don't understand, he said, looking at her face and the face of the woman in the picture, I don't understand, Bethany. Why does this face look so different from yours? I've been trying for hours now, but I always end up with the same face. Will you sit for me, if you aren't too sleepy? I can't rest until I get this portrait correct. He took a palette knife to scrape paint away from Carolynn's nose and cheeks.

'Stop, I said to him. Don't do that. Leave it as it is. But, he said, I want to paint a picture of us. This doesn't look like you at all. We stood there puzzled. I guess I can't really paint that well, he said. But look at your face, I told him, look how perfect it is. You are a fabulous painter, I said, you shouldn't sell yourself short. Maybe I am just like how you've painted me. Bethany, he said, I don't understand this. I really thought I could paint you from memory. But it is a fine painting otherwise, don't you think, he said. Of course, it is, I said. Don't worry about my face. I'm sure people will know it is me. Maybe the paint needs to dry a little, I said. You know how sometimes things shrink when they dry?'

He just shook his head and looked at the mist outside the window. She put her arm around him and took the brush. 'Come to bed,' she said. 'I'll sit for you tomorrow.'

And she did, the next day. He scraped the nose and the cheeks out and re-did them, perfectly. It was Bethany and him now, naked, looking at the viewer. A beautiful painting, alive, worthy of being hung in the hallway. But something changed that day, after he finished the portrait. He told her that he was tired, tired in the bones, and that he wanted to go away on a holiday where he could soak in a hot-water spring. 'Wherever you want,' she said as she put away the stack of dishes just out of the dishwasher. 'If you want, we can take the car and leave right now.'

'I want to go alone,' he said. 'I'm not trying to avoid you, but I can't get over Rebecca's death. I need to put her to rest, in peace, inside myself. I need to meet her, just father and daughter, so that we can sort this thing out, this grief she has left me with.'

That's how they parted, Bethany and her husband. He returned after three months. Something had changed between them. They gave it an honest go, waited for another moment of togetherness, but after another four months, it seemed clear there was nowhere forward to move. Not that they didn't still do the same things they had always done— they made love with the same passion and frequency, they went out and met his friends, he painted her from memory, again and again, Bethany on thirteen canvases, but the stone of their union, the pit and core, had vanished. He waited in bed one morning for her to come out of the shower. She had always changed in front of him, hiding nothing. But on that morning she turned away from him, towards the curtained window, ever so slightly, as she put on her bra. Of course he didn't mention it, but it rankled her that she had done that—a part of her mind had pushed her to hide her breasts from him. He called her to his side, took and kissed her hand, and asked her if she still felt they had a life together to share. They divorced at the end of summer, before the holiday season. He bought real estate for her all over the Bay Area because she didn't want to discuss money. You know I'll always love you, he told her. You know you can always count on me.

Carolynn went back to Doctor Schwartz with a face in mind. She changed her name back to Carolynn and moved to San Rafael. There was no question of going back to her ex-husband now that she'd done away with the face with which he'd fallen in love. In any case, he could paint her from memory now. She went to an exhibition of his paintings once, a small gallery on Turk Street, where solemn people admired thirteen different paintings in which Bethany appeared in various guises. He was standing before their family portrait. She wanted to go and touch him, to smooth his hair and take his face in her hands, but her knees started to shake. She left without talking to him. 'What would I have said?' Carolynn said. 'I wonder if he would've recognized me. I looked so different by then.' That was face number three on the wall.

'And your second husband?' I asked.

'Oh, he was an asshole. I met him at a real estate seminar. He had charm, you know, the smart salesman. He was loud but he made me feel like I was the centre of his world. He'd take me to the movies and feel me up. It felt cheap, how he touched me sometimes, but he could be incredibly sweet, too. I thought I could change him, you know, into being nice all the time. I knew he was an alcoholic before I married him, but I thought I could change that, too. It felt like a challenge. I thought, If I am woman enough, he'll change for me. That pig. He cheated on me and started selling my clients to his friends. Three months is how long that lousy marriage lasted. I had to wait for another three months before I could file for divorce. He wanted to work it out, but I was out of there. No more marriage for me. If I find a decent guy who'll love me, I'll share my life with him, but the institution of marriage and I have irreconcilable differences now.'

Back to Doctor Schwartz again. Carolynn no longer thought it was possible to have one perfect face, but the doctor convinced her that there were many, many perfect faces. Why give up now? And there were a few things Carolynn wanted changed. Why don't you change your chin, the doctor asked. Men like interesting chins. Carolynn thought about that for over two months. She thought of how men looked when their faces were close to her, when they hovered above her. When she was alone, she'd play them back from the vault of her memory, flickers of changing faces in various stages of adoration and grimace. Therefore the chin in picture number four.

'And five?' I asked. She slid down into the bed. I cracked my neck and she made a sound as if that were painful. I took off my belt and undid my shirt-cuffs.

'Do you want some water?' she asked.

'Yes, but I want to hear about picture number five,' I said after her.

She returned with a pitcher of water and a couple of glasses. She went back to the kitchen and returned with a chilled bottle of gin and fixed two drinks.

'What about picture number five?' I asked her. I had taken a chair while she sat on the bed, her knees folded under her. She smiled, but said nothing more. I finished the gin quickly, stood to stretch my legs, and examined the pictures, lingering on each face. Bethany was by far the happiest of the lot; her eyes had a light in them which the other faces lacked. I sat next to Carolynn and we kissed. It was a lingering kiss all done by the neck and lips; she held her glass of gin just out of the way. I kissed the corners of her mouth.

'That face didn't come from Muriel. I didn't get another surgery after the fourth. For some reason, my chin changed overnight, and the implants in my cheeks started to fall.'

I unbuttoned her shirt. She continued to talk as we undressed each other delicately, greeting the preciousness of our selves. 'You are beautiful,' I said and touched her collarbone.

'I moved to Santa Rosa and took that office on B Street. Everything worked fine for a few months. I took on three more girls to work for me. I did all the actual selling, but they brought in leads and kept the office, processed loans and so on. I didn't want to get back into dating so soon. I guess you could say I got burned, so I took my time.

'One afternoon, I return to the office after lunch, Juanita goes, Can I help you? I thought she was trying to be funny. She hadn't seen me in the morning because she was out running an errand, so she must be teasing me, I thought. Oh shut up, Juanita, I said, did anyone call for me?

'Then she stands up and walks to me. Sorry, she says, Do you have an appointment? I told her to quit joking. I walked towards my office. Excuse me, she says, I'd be happy to help you. Are you scheduled to meet with Ms Flint?'

'It's me, Juanita, I tell her. 'Carolynn!' Her face became pale. What's wrong, Juanita? I asked.

'What's wrong with you, Carolynn? she asked back. What happened to you? I knew she wasn't joking anymore. Nobody jokes in a tone like that. What's wrong? I asked. I only had a beer. Maybe I'm red, I said.

'No, she said and grabbed my hand and pulled me to the bathroom. Look, she said, look in the mirror.'

The sudden change of face, as it were, created a host of problems. Carolynn had to recall all the advertisements she had put in local papers because they all had face number four on them. The clients with whom she had met few days before hesitated to do business with Juanita. She never contacted the one she'd lunched with because she could never be sure which face it had been. Face number four was on her driving license and in the office literature and business cards she had distributed up and down the Sonoma coast and in the city. Her neighbours called the cops after seeing face number five enter and leave the house while face number four had disappeared without a trace. She had to take a DNA test to prove that she was Carolynn Flint. She switched houses after that and moved into the one where I sat beside her, listening to this bizarre story.

Now her face changed every few days, shifting without any warning, like light reflecting off a disturbed lake. She could be driving to the grocery and she'd check her reflection in the rear-view mirror and it would be a different person. Once, she went to her gynaecologist, who had to leave the examination room briefly. When she returned, she saw Carolynn, checked the room, even behind the door, and ran out to find Carolynn. Of course, she couldn't go to her parents' home anymore. If she stood before a mirror and concentrated, she could get her face to return to normal. But there was no telling how long it'd stay that way. Every few days it would settle into that shape again, like water finding its natural place in a stone sculpted by rain.

'How would you feel,' she asked me, 'if I wake up with a different face tomorrow?'

'We'll have to see, won't we?' I said. We were very gentle that night, as if a lifetime of acquaintance had passed between us. We both smiled a lot—wide, sunny smiles— as we searched each other, the unchanging face of mine, and the sliding, morphing face of hers.

I saw Carolynn frequently after that. I told Basu about her. He wouldn't believe the story at first, but I guess it was harder for him to believe that I was seeing so many different women in a week. Carolynn and I agreed to not meet each other's friends—there was no point to it. We'd be sitting in a corner in a bar or in the park and her face would start to reconfigure itself. She learned to recognize the look on my face when I watched her change. I'd kiss every new feature that appeared and disappeared on her face.

I felt jealous at times, or something akin to it, when I sat waiting for her and she was late. What if that woman in the corner is her, I'd think, what if she sits and flirts with other men, goes to the bathroom and puts on her face and comes to me? What if we are like the tops of trees, swaying in the wind and coming close to each other then separating before

we make contact because she wore the face of a stranger
while I scanned the crowd? But I learned to recognize her
by and by, from the vocabulary of the body and its gestures,
from how her hand reached for something or how she
shook her hair and smoothed it over to one side when a
new song came on. Through all of this her eyes remained
unchanged. I found myself repeating the old habit of kissing
the shoulder in sleep and knowing the eyes that opened
briefly to look at me. I'd bring her flowers, and wine when I
could afford a good bottle, and we'd sit with our arms
around each other, watching the sky change colours. Did I
ever fall in love with her? No. I don't think I did. I don't
think she fell in love with me either. But if there is a word
for what existed between us, inside each for the other, I
don't know that word yet.

I'd occasionally take the Number 80 bus to San Francisco,
from there to go to Stanford to visit Mithun or to San
Mateo to visit Tuan. We'd go to a movie together or cook
at Mithun's apartment in Stanford, steal oranges or
persimmons from the trees on campus. If Tuan and I
happened to be in San Francisco, we'd find a bar or end up
at a club on Broadway.

Tuan had just returned from Vietnam, after a visit to the
village of his birth and rural childhood—not at all different
to my own childhood in Khaireni, from where we carried

memories of rice paddies and dragonflies and buffalos and hot summers with fierce rains. We met in the city, ate in Chinatown, walked along the piers. We chanced upon the Beat Museum, a bookshop full of memorabilia from the Beat Generation. Tuan and I took a photo under the mural of Neil Cassidy and Jack Kerouac. I doubt if the photo exists anymore. We found a Korean bar where people still smoked inside. Afterwards, we went to the Mitchell Brothers' Theatre on O'Farrell Street. After saying goodbye to Tuan, I sat by the fountain near the U.N. Building on Market. The Number 80 to Santa Rosa stopped on Market and Seventh, but the crowd was more interesting near the fountain.

I was smoking the cigarette Tuan left with me when I saw Heather smile at me as she walked past. She didn't stop. I remembered that her parents were retiring to San Francisco—not the city proper, but somewhere nearby. Or it could have been the city. It was either in Marin County or in the Marina; it had been a long time since Heather had told me about their new house in California, so I couldn't recall. Heather hadn't smiled at me as she would, I mean as she would smile at me in particular, with the baggage of love and the ruins of it. Sure, I had changed since Walla Walla. That was inevitable. Being with Carolynn meant taking better care of my appearance, too: now I looked less youthful but better put together. Did Heather mistake me for somebody else? I watched her walk away, not a drop of the old mournfulness absent from the slow stride, the hair long again and lustrous, catching the sun as it always did.

Strings descended from above the skyscrapers to pick and puppet me along—I have no other way of explaining the sudden pang that solidified in my chest and made me follow her. I found a whole lot of things that had been left unsaid and now needed attention, settlement, closure, however you put it. I walked faster to close the gap between us. She could cross the street and a red light could catch me, and with that small urban tragedy I could lose this moment forever. I might never see her again, unless I tried to track her down through Whitman's alumni association. Which I wouldn't do.

'Heather,' I called. But my voice cracked and even I could barely hear the name. I hurried, trying to look inconspicuous, trying to get to her side. If I could surprise her, I thought. I remembered how she'd always hugged me, with honesty, her eyes shut and hands reaching around to my shoulder blades, rubbing my spine while she murmured something like 'How have you been?' and 'Why didn't you call?' She always murmured, as if it was less important for me to hear than it was for her to say it. 'Heather,' I called again. She didn't turn.

By now I was convinced that she was doing this on purpose. She did smile at me, I thought. It must make her happy her to see me. But she is still angry about something. I never said goodbye to her after graduation, when everybody was hugging each other and exchanging congratulatory cards. In any case, we'd lost touch over the last semester. She must be angry about that, I thought, She must be upset I haven't written to her since. Then that made me angry: it wasn't as if I hadn't been thinking of her. I wouldn't go so far as to say I missed her, but I might have, were I honest enough to admit it to myself. I searched for her shawl and turquoise bag. She was standing on the escalator, descending into the Civic Center BART Station.

I was right behind her when Heather's mobile phone rang. 'Hello,' she said. It was her. I knew that voice. I could follow that voice into a dark cave and find her mouth with mine. I waited for her to finish talking. We were walking towards the turnstiles now. I didn't have a ticket, didn't have a need for one, so I reached and touched her elbow. She looked back.

It wasn't her. It wasn't Heather.

'Yes?' she said, looking me up and down. She had Heather's eyes, but everything else was somebody else's. The voice now sounded different. When I was certain that she was Heather, she had sounded like Heather, but now she was somebody else. There was no mistaking it.

'I am sorry,' I said. She became suspicious—perhaps my face changed, perhaps the grin on my face disappeared as if I was guilty of something profane, and she thought I was being weird. 'I am sorry,' I said again. 'I thought you were a friend. I mean someone I knew. I thought you were Heather.'

'Well, I am not Heather,' she said. She said the name as if it were poison. The girl turned and fed her ticket into the machine. The gate opened. And, just like that, she was on the other side.

She turned once to look at me. I stood there, feeling foolish and disappointed. A fist caught my inside and slowly pushed it up to my throat. I turned and walked to the escalators, taking deep breaths. I had wanted to tell Heather everything that had been left unsaid and see in her all the things I longed to look at again. I had so desperately wanted it to be her that everything I wanted to say to her tried to escape me anyway. I struggled out of the station, grabbing onto the evening sun and air outside to avoid sinking back. Why couldn't it have been Heather? What had I done to deserve such violence?

I still think of Heather sometimes, as I do of Carolynn, but until then, the woman I loved, if I loved anyone at all, was Heather. My relationship with Carolynn lasted longer and, in some ways, changed the least. Whereas with Heather, a relationship that had started without much of a drama—no grand courting, no grand parting—had ended in something akin to violence. I didn't call her for a few days after that night when we'd fought for the first time and slept through the night with barely an inch of skin touching each other. She'd said something like 'I need some space,' and I'd replied, 'You can have your space and your time.' The next morning I'd rolled out of bed and dressed while she propped herself on her elbows and waited for something. I'd gone out of the door without looking back or kissing her. Three days after that—I think it was a Friday evening—I had gone back to her room. It was unlocked. Inside, her blue fishnet stockings were thrown on the floor.

Heather sat on her bed that evening, facing the window, making yarn on her spinning wheel. I went in and sat on the bed, behind her. We had never really fought before, so I didn't know what I was supposed to do. I had decided against taking flowers or a six-pack of beer: I thought simple talk should be enough, the simple love between us would be enough. She kept looking out of the window. I put my head on the pillow and looked at the ceiling. She turned and said, 'I have something to tell you.'

'What?' I asked.

'I cheated on you. Yesterday.' Her voice wavered.

'Thank you,' I said. The response came very naturally. I guess I meant to say, Look what you've done: ruined a perfectly good thing over an evening's quarrel. Thanks to you, it is all gone now; it'll never be the same again. But 'thank you' is never the response to give at a time like that! Thank you for cheating on me, because you know I have been cheating on you all along, and now we are even? Thank you for making me feel less guilty? It was my turn to go and sit by the window.

'Say something,' she said. 'Hit me if you want.'

'Where the fuck do you get these ideas about me?' I yelled. 'You really think I'd hit you?'

'No,' she said. 'I just don't want you to act like nothing happened.'

'Oh,' I said, 'something happened, all right. A big fucking thing happened.'

Thereafter reigned a silence fifteen minutes long.

And then I said something she finally found unforgivable. 'Did you have fun?' I said.

Now that I think back, I am convinced that the same thing would have led to different results if I had said it differently, at some other time in the night. If it had been, say, after an hour of further quarrelling and crying—yes, I would've cried with her—or, with her face in my hands and a twinkle of mischief in my eyes, things could have been different. But it felt like the rug had been pulled from under my feet, like I was walking on air and any second I'd plunge thousands of miles into nothingness like…yes, like I had been cheated upon. I was angry—at myself, at her, at the guy, whoever the fuck it was. Such beautiful months I'd spent with her. We'd made love under that very window; I'd kissed her neck and hair in the light that filtered in; her cat, Midnight, was dying and I helped her take care of it; and now it was all over after an evening's quarrel. We drifted apart over our final year in college. I managed to become a bitter drunk, which some damaged women found attractive. Who was I to complain?

The time came for me to return to Kathmandu, to chase the foolish pipe dream of becoming a writer. I was still broke—as if I had treated penury as a prerequisite for a creative life. Basu drove me to the airport when it was time for me to return to Nepal. Carolynn came with us. When her face changed on the way to the airport, Basu smiled. Mithun couldn't make it to the airport, as I had expected—he had too much work in the lab. 'I'll see you in Kathmandu,' he said. Tuan was at work in the city, so we picked him up for the trip to the airport. Carolynn and I sat in the back, holding hands, whispering about the possibility of her visiting me in Kathmandu. At the terminal, Tuan and Basu let me spend a few minutes alone with Carolynn, who ran off to the parking lot after a long, tight hug, leaving me to say my goodbyes to the boys.

If I had to say what I have learned from life so far, I wouldn't be able to write a single word of truth: I'd likely ramble on and on, but never manage to say anything of substance. I don't think I have learned anything about people, much less about women, or love. I still remember how hard it was to say goodbye to Carolynn, the woman of a thousand faces, the woman I never loved, and I remember how easily everything ended with Heather, whom I did love, with however much of it I could muster. I had thought leaving Walla Walla would be difficult to do but, as it turned out, leaving Santa Rosa was harder. I still wonder if Heather lives on a fishing boat off the coast of Alaska, or what Carolynn looks like in the morning. I wonder what the crowd looks like in the brew pub and who must live in the apartment near the park in Walla Walla where Heather lived when she still loved me. I don't think I'll ever return to either of the places, but I'll think of the women for a long time to come.

THE VANISHING ACT

I was waiting for Basu at Julliard Park in downtown Santa Rosa when it started drizzling. He was coming from the Mexican store with a roast chicken and beer. I figured he'd find me under the gazebo because the bench by the pond where we'd decided to eat a picnic dinner would be wet. A woman out running in the night waved at me, but I'd forgotten my glasses again that evening, and although I waved back, I didn't greet her with a name. After a minute, a tall man wearing a white hat and a light turquoise tuxedo came out of the dark, carrying a sack over his shoulder. He put the sack down on the only other bench under the gazebo. The glow from a sensuously curved pipe lit up his nose punched to the left. He took off his hat, checked me out, and tapped the pipe against the bench. Two quick taps, then another.

The sack sighed, then rustled. A gnarled pair of hands folded the mouth of the sack down around a bald head. A baseball hat found its fit on the head. A tired dwarf squirmed on the bench until the sack fell to the ground. A circus clown without the red nose. All the trappings of a jester straight out of a deck of cards.

'Hey, man!' said the clown. He was calm. 'You speak English? You Mexican?'

'No,' I said.

'We're Mexican,' he said. The tall man nodded, then stood up startled and picked the sack, ready to push it over the clown's head. I raised a hand to stop him: it was only Basu, jogging through the rain. 'That's my friend,' I said. 'It's cool.'

Basu froze three paces from the gazebo. A man in a tuxedo, a clown in a baseball hat and a sack. 'It's cool,' I said to Basu in English, 'they're cool.'

'You got food?' said the clown. Basu hesitated with the grocery bags. 'That from the Mexican store?' The clown pointed at the bags. Without waiting for confirmation, he let out a whistle in appreciation. 'Bet you I could guess what's in the bags,' he said.

I laughed. Basu was still trying to figure out what was going on. He hadn't yet slipped into Nepali to ask who they were. 'Once you seen the bags, anybody can guess,' I said.

'Whooey!' The clown rubbed his hands. 'Bet you got hot chicken and cold cervezas in there.'

Basu's eyebrows were still doing the snake dance of WTF! He is the more gregarious of us, but he doesn't take to surprises very well. If the world around him is clearly defined, he will choose to waltz through it. If there is a pebble in his dancing shoes, he will hobble around waiting for attention until I or Adele grab him by the shoulder, tell him to take his shoes off and move on. If he'd been the one waiting under the gazebo, he'd be telling me the story of their encounter, in Nepali to better pepper it with the slang of our boyhood years.

'Bet you got hot chicken and cold cervezas in there,' the clown said again. A whole roasted chicken between two would make a decent meal. But between four? That, too, the silent one being a giant of a Mexican. 'Yeah, yeah,' said the clown. 'You boys ain't got enough to share.'

'No, no,' said Basu, quartering the chicken with his hands. The flimsy plastic forks that came with the food were a joke. I cracked open two Dos Equis for the Mexicans.

'Man, you guys are awesome,' said the clown. The giant offered Basu his fist to bump. Nobody said a word until the chicken was all gone, even the bones gnawed on and sucked dry.

It was raining harder. There was no light in the gazebo. Long shadows cast by the trees around the park criss-crossed over the wet grass and made the rain look like sharp glass pins darting into the ground. Automated sprinklers still poked out to add to the warm summer rain.

'Your friend is huge,' I said to the clown.

'Luchadore.' The clown was proud of the giant. A masked wrestler. The giant grinned, dug out a silk mask in white, gold and crimson. But he didn't wear it.

'You guys a bunch of runaways from a Mexican circus?' I asked. Basu giggled.

'Yeah, man,' the clown wiped his bald head and flopped the hat back on. 'That we are.'

'Why'd you run away? Tired of being shot out of a cannon?' I said.

'Got tired of getting shoved into the old elephant's ass,' the clown said, making a farting noise, flailing one arm like an elephant's trunk, pinching his nose with the other. The giant roared with laughter. When the clown removed his hand, his nose had begotten its necessary accessory: the red bulb. After shaking his head without any exaggerated sadness, the clown removed the red bulb.

'Got tired of it,' he said. 'My brother—he is too simple to make it outside the ring. Me, I'm too evil to make it in the ring.'

Basu offered the Mexicans his pouch of tobacco. The giant refilled his pipe. 'I wanted to do magic,' said the clown, 'but Xander, the boss man, he don't let nobody else do magic.'

'Know any tricks?' asked Basu.

'I don't do tricks, man!' said the clown. 'I do magic!'

He punched the giant's arm and said something like silencio. The giant nodded, patted down the empty sack and prepared it for the clown. The giant looked at his watch and grunted a go-ahead.

'This magic lasts only as long as I can hold my breath. But you guys are going to love this one,' the clown said. He stepped into the sack on the bench and pulled it over his head. The giant pursed the mouth of the sack and lifted it off the bench, but the sack did not sag, nor did it seem to possess any added weight. The giant rolled the sack into a bundle smaller than a loaf of bread from Rosita's. The clown had vanished, into the sack, into thin air. When the giant handed the rolled-up sack to Basu, his eyebrows became even more serpentine.

The giant checked his watch, unfurled the sack with a smart snap, stood it to its height and opened it. The clown pulled the sack down around him. He slid down to sit on the bench, waist-deep in the sack. His bald head shone with sweat, and he was out of breath.

'One of these days, I'm going to hold my breath forever,' he said. 'When they come knocking on the door, looking for me, to stuff me into a cannon and shoot me back to my old life, I'm going to hold my breath forever.'

'Have another beer,' said Basu. 'This is good beer.' It was still raining around us, and the sprinklers were still spewing in their epileptic fits, spraying into the clean rain.

Of course, all magic is tricks. That night, around the time when Jon Stewart came on, Adele called Basu from Boston because she couldn't sleep. Basu described the clown and his trick to Adele, but she wouldn't believe him: the rain, the chicken and the beer, the clown and the giant, the sack, the magic. He ran downstairs, made me turn down the volume on the TV and answer Adele's questions. She made me answer in yes or no: did the sack really fold up to the size of a bread loaf? Yes. Do you think it was a trick? No. Really? You don't think it was a trick? I guess, it could've been, but. Yes or no? No, I'd say no. Did the clown actually carry the giant away in the sack afterwards? No! It was the other way around. Basu lied.

That was also the first summer of my being shot out of a cannon without a net to catch me. The woman I had been in love with for years decided that she loved her husband more. I was jobless, sleeping in Basu's broom closet under the stairs. If I wasn't out looking for a job, I'd spend entire days before the TV, going out at midday to read my shadow on the porch. Sometimes, between two and four in the afternoon, Bhim dai from Apartment 9 would come downstairs and we'd watch DVDs of Hindi movies rented from an Indian convenience store up the street.

The day after meeting the Mexicans, Bhim dai brought Satyajit Ray's *The Chess Players*. But he seemed preoccupied; he kept standing up from the couch only to sit down again. Before we could finish the movie, Bhim dai had to go to Curry Land, where he was the chef. Around nine Basu called to say I should meet him at The Belvedere, where Basu usually played pool while we drank away the money he'd earned in tips that evening. I was chatting up Manny, the bouncer, when a man lingered by my side, then went in. Basu chalked up his name to play pool and came out to roll cigarettes in the yard. The man who had lingered outside came to the yard and lingered again.

'Excuse me,' he said, 'are you from India?' Basu's eyebrows started twitching; he slinked away to another corner.

'Why?' I asked the man in Nepali.

'Eh! You're Nepali!' he said. He seemed at once relieved and perplexed. 'Sujit,' he said. We shook hands. I called Basu over, they shook hands. Turns out, Sujit was Bhim dai's son, come into town that morning after quitting a job in Indiana. Bhim dai had been fighting with him for the past month, asking Sujit to move to Santa Rosa. 'It's not hard finding a job here, I guess,' he said. I smiled and raised my beer.

Basu and I had a lot in common with Sujit: boarding-school teenage years in Kathmandu, the search for American universities with decent scholarships. Four years later, out in the job market, searching for an employer who'd put us in the permanent residency way. Sujit had degrees in maths and economics and wanted to move to New York but had fallen into a comfortable actuary job with a company that specialized in insuring wheat and corn crops. But, unlike us, when he came to the U.S., his father had been there for seven years. They had both been bachelors in the country: Sujit moved from one inexpensive college to another, eventually soul-searching through different departments at Indiana University, while Bhim dai moved from one new Indian restaurant to the next, up and down the West Coast, enticed by half a dollar's rise in pay and climate that his ageing bones could tolerate.

I'd never see Sujit around the apartment complex, but he

and I frequently ran into each other around the copy-
machine in the Junior College library, or at The Belvedere
in the evenings. One fine Sunday afternoon, I was walking
through the park. Young couples were lolling about on the
grass, waiting for their show-time at the theatre. Sujit was
sitting exactly where the Mexican giant had sat so many
days ago.

'I don't know,' he started. 'The pay is all right, but the
work isn't something I'd want to do for long.' At least you
have a job, I said. He said he'd buy me drinks that evening.
But I didn't go out that evening. While walking home, I
had found a story that wanted to be told—about a woman
who has had too many cosmetic surgeries on her face, so
that her face now changed with a will of its own. Basu
called from The Belvedere, Sujit took his phone to call me
out to the bar, but I was just hitting my stride with a story I
had been trying to write for the past month, and finally
something was happening, so I didn't want to go out. I was
already asleep when Basu came home.

Around midnight, Sandesh, who lived next door and
waited at Curry Land, knocked on our door. He was sitting
on the steps, typing furiously on his phone, still wearing his
black bow tie, his shirt tails hanging out.

'Bhim dai asked for you,' he said. 'I can't find Sujit dai. I
don't have his number.' I didn't have Sujit's number either.
I woke Basu up for his car keys. Sandesh drove me to the
hospital. A helicopter ambulance was taking off from the
roof when Sandesh dropped me off outside the emergency

ward. A nurse tapping her nails on the enquiry counter looked up and asked, 'You from Nepal?' Yes. 'Family?' No. Neighbour.

'He said he has a son?' she asked, reading me from head to toe, a bit worried.

'I can't reach him. Don't have his number.' She took to tapping a pencil on the counter. 'He got a job today, went to the bar to celebrate, didn't come home.' I shrugged.

'Is this you?' she asked. Bhim dai had written my name on a piece of paper. Sandesh had written his name under it. I showed the nurse my college ID and my Washington State ID. She started walking.

This was Bhim dai's second stroke. The first had come after a week-long fever. He had been trying to dress to go back to work, although everybody else told him he should rest for a couple more days. He had staggered into the kitchen in Apartment 9, gasping for breath, trying to reach the sink. Norbu, two-time Everest summiteer and the naan chef at Curry Land, had called 911, digging Bhim dai into a debt hole from which he was only now slowly climbing out. Now, the second stroke. Sandesh had told me how it happened: Bhim dai was in the prep-kitchen, preparing the sauce for a masala curry. He had fallen forward and, in grabbing the pan for support, had poured the ghee and onion all over his shirt. The ghee had caught on fire. If he had been alone in the prep kitchen, he could have burned the place down.

He was moving his fingers, one after the other, when I

walked to his bedside. The plastic chair on his side of the room had a lunch box on it, so I sat on the bed. He closed his eyes after blinking hard to focus on my face. He pushed the tip of his tongue out just a little to cough gently, but kept his eyes closed. When I saw tears roll down the corner of his eyes, I patted his hand.

'Bhim dai,' I said, 'I am here. You called for me?'

'I know,' he said in English. This was the first time Bhim dai had spoken to me in the language. 'Can you find my son for me?' he asked.

'I'll try. I don't have his number.'

'Where are my clothes? My phone should be in there somewhere.' I told him to not worry. The worst was over, and Sujit was out celebrating his new job. Now father and son could live together in peace, I said. Bhim dai tried to laugh, but it made him sound wounded, pierced through.

'Open the box.' He pointed to the lunch box. A fruit salad, a piece of bread, yogurt. Bhim dai laughed. 'Fruit salad, every day, fruit salad for a year now. And still this happens.' Chefs at curry restaurants are malnourished, underpaid, overstressed, overworked, and fed two meals a day of their own cooking. Salt, spices, ghee, meat. The perfect recipe for an early stroke, Bhim dai said. He had been eating his own cooking for the past eleven years. While slowly cutting himself off from his guthi and clansmen in Patan, while corrupting the silk tether between father and son. Now, with a year of fruit salad and the son back under the same roof, this. The second stroke.

'My son,' Bhim dai started, then stalled to gather his thoughts. 'My son doesn't want to live with me,' he said. 'He can't do it, he says. So many years of living on his own. Hostel for so long. His mother died two months after I became illegal here. I couldn't go back. Ashamed. Now he is ashamed of me, ashamed to live under the same room.

'He talks to me in English,' he said. 'I know he wants to say something, to talk, but he can't do it without saying it in English.' I massaged his hands. We were a couple of quiet men who enjoyed old Hindi movies, who appreciated each other's capacity for quietude. And here I was, trying to supply him with expressed emotions through small, firm circles kneaded into his palms. What did he need from his apartment, I asked him.

'Nothing,' he said, 'there is nothing there.'

Bhim dai didn't want me to stay the night watching over him. Hospital regulations did not permit it in any case. I walked back to 915 Mendocino. Sujit was smoking under a pine tree by the driveway. He gave me his cigarette. 'How is my father?' he asked.

'This is his second stroke,' I said.

'I know,' he said. 'I was across the street, at the Italian place, when the ambulance came for him. I should have gone with him.' But he didn't know how to do that. What would he say to his father? What would he do at the hospital when they'd ask for Bhim dai's insurance papers, or for his work permit? 'That makes me sound so petty,' he said. He crushed pine needles on his palm. I gave him the cigarette.

'He is fine now,' I said. Bhim dai would survive, he would continue making himself fruit salad for lunch and dinner. He would move on to work for any new Indian restaurant that he could take a bus to.

'When Mother died,' Sujit said, 'I kept thinking of Father, all alone in this country. He didn't even have a phone number then. I kept thinking of what I would say when I'd get to talk to him.'

Bhim dai returned to 915 Mendocino after a week in the hospital. Every day, he would come downstairs, make chapati and simple curries for us. We'd watch movies. He became talkative, speaking in English more often than in Nepali, telling me stories about watching movies at Ashok Hall and Ranjana, about passing letters to Sujit's mother when she started working in a bank in Pulchowk. We never talked about Sujit. I didn't tell him that his son had been across the street from Curry Land when he'd had the second stroke.

Six weeks after the stroke, Bhim dai and I watched Ray's *Apur Sansar*. He cried watching the bit after Sharmila Tagore's death, so we watched Apu's wanderings again: when he is in the forest, with Ravi Shankar's flute picking up the strains of his loss, up to when Apu commits his novel to the wind, by the sea.

Bhim dai left town the next day, to vanish into the American mass. I never returned to Sujit the DVD his father left behind, which tells the story of another father desperately trying to erase his track from the sands of time, walking to the endless sea where he can scatter the shells of his former life. A year after Bhim dai's disappearance, Basu wrote to tell me that Sujit has moved out of 915 Mendocino—just as Basu and Adele have moved out and started a life together. On their kitchen wall is a frame with a flyer for a Mexican circus and portraits cut from the missing persons posters we found stapled to the utility pole outside 915 Mendocino. Two men stare glumly at us—one a dwarf, the other a giant, long vanished into the breathing world.

THE CONDOLENCE PICTURE

It was a teahouse in the mountains, no more than a thin, cold sponge mattress and plywood walls plastered with newspaper, a door cut into a wall as if a passage out of the mountains. The air was rare and damp with fog. Nobody laughed up here—travellers worn thin from the climb find no reason to laugh. Cold air pelted the windows, fog pearled on the panes. Feet dragged and shuffled through the passage, haunches groaned onto beds: a day was won, another waited. These were the sounds of the teahouse. Even the door latch was frozen into a metallic cold to discourage people from leaving their rooms. Some wretch had carried enough newspapers over at least thirteen days of mountain walking to plaster every inch of plywood in the teahouse. This was no refuge after a hard day's climb, but a burial place for cheer.

Darkness was far from falling but, when it would come, it would pour into the tiny valley like a rain of soot. A sky

pricked with stars would light up the powdered heads of
Himalayan peaks once the fog soaked back into the air. But
that was still another hour away. Between now and then
was the numbness of waiting, already, for the sun that
would perhaps rise, its first fiery dazzle on the snow the
warmest promise any day can bring. The knife-blade of the
air cut through defences—coat, cardigan, shirt, another
shirt, warm underwear—to bore into the body's frail purse
of warmth. I shivered from sitting still, from sitting with a
still thought, and jumped up with a whoop! Somebody
coughed in the next room and dropped a heavy trekking
boot to the floor.

Head curled to the knees, I huffed and shivered to warm
the toes, but the sponge of the mattress and the nylon of
the sleeping bag soaked away all warmth. It was futile to
demand sleep. I thought I'd read a bit, but it was hard to
breach into the page and inhabit the story. I was cracking
my knuckles behind my head when I saw Sparrow's face on
the wall. Above the pillow, and repeated, replicated,
patterned like a fractal design, over the toes, across the
room, all over the door: the same face, Sparrow squinting
at the world, surprised to catch me in his gaze. Sparrow
garlanded by thick-set words and two discrete dates.
Sparrow smiling in pitted print, but Sparrow dead, gone
without consequence.

It couldn't be!

Childhood has a different name, a different face not shown to everyone who tries to open that tight fist of things not easily abandoned to the tides of time. Sparrow was one of the things that I had never dared whisper of—I'd refused to tell stories about him, refused to have his spectre settle among the new friends I've made over these long years. He was already being called Sparrow when I met him. He was already that shirt and skin of bones, scurrying from one place to another because everyday gravity failed entirely to slow him down.

As a child, his teeth had tried to escape the gates of his lips. Through his teenage years he had talked through an ugly wire mesh. When he finally got rid of them, just before passing high school, his teeth had aligned into a smile he wouldn't stop flashing at everything. But, throughout, he remained Sparrow.

And just like that, he was gone. Disappeared. Sparrow had decided his friends were of no consequence to him. He had chosen a life, with his lean frame and filed smile, forged away from the past, absent of anyone who had known him before the escape. We heard of him intermittently, of his chance encounters, tales about him filtering down through many an ear—Sparrow disappointing hard-earned appointments, Sparrow achieving successes of the undeserved sort. But he wouldn't respond to our emails, he never posted a photo of himself, and nobody wrote about him. In our minds, Sparrow let himself get watered thin into nobody. By and by, we didn't think of him anymore:

we, his friends. We learned to move on, unaffected by his absence.

Carefully, I tore out a square from the panel by the pillow and folded it into the copy of *The Idiot* which I had schlepped to the highest altitude I was ever to climb. But sleep didn't come easy, not even when I spent a good twenty minutes staring at the bare patch on the plywood partition. The moon sank behind yet another mountain.

When we were young, we called him Sparrow because he was like one. When we were young, when we were in school, when we were *small*—phrases that insist it was a different world then, a different moral planet, that seek to absolve us from the natural cruelties we practiced upon each other and upon ourselves. Sparrow would be so tired after being bullied and chased and run off on errands that he slept like one dead, so that, at midnight, when the House Master no longer walked the corridors, we would lift the bed and Sparrow and leave the bed in the garden outside the House. A guard would wake him sometimes; then the guard would wake the House Master, who'd wake the prefects, who would then wake us up for a few laps around the football pitch and cold showers after. But it was more natural for Sparrow to sleep in the garden right through the night, to wake to the sheen of moisture on his face and dew on the blanket. He would come into the dormitory as if nothing had happened at all and politely ask another boy—often the same two-faced friend of his who had carried him out to the garden in the middle of the night—to help him quietly carry in the bed.

The next day was all downhill. Air came home to the lungs and the feet found their rhythm and holds. A river roared below the path, goading the body down the valley and out, out again into gorges scented with pine mulch and the musk of highland flowers, out into thicker air and mellower light. The earth around the path darkened and thickened and buzzed with insects and many more birds flitted between trees. I had been running too fast to not get shaky knees. When I nearly snapped an ankle and slid off the path into the blue air below, I smiled to the broad sky and sat down to drink some water and rest.

I had a mind to commit Sparrow to the breeze, to see shreds of him flutter away over the river, nest among pine cones and tangle in juniper shrubs. But when I read the words again, I couldn't part with the scrap. Sparrow smiled with his straight, filed teeth. Under his photo, these words:

> Holding a pear to his chest, begging his wife Chetana to hold his hand, Niranjan died on the evening of September 13th, 2006. Friends, mourn if you loved him any. His family mourns.

Holding a pear to his chest! Begging his wife to hold his hand! I immediately envied Sparrow's deathbed tableau and despised it. It seemed vulgarly perfected. It begged for approval. It involved a pear held to the chest!

I hadn't noticed the quiet, wiry man behind me, breathing with some effort, leaning his chin on a tall walking stick and swaying to let loose sweat beads from a scraggly beard. 'Will I get there by four?' he asked.

'Hajur?' I asked.

'I should get there by four, no?' he said. Too perplexed to answer, I nodded and smiled. Reach where? There was many a rest stop along the trail. He shared his appreciation of the view, I shared my water with him. I didn't ask how far up the mountain he intended to go. 'Walk slowly,' I said, and ran downhill, leaving him alone amidst birdcalls and mule droppings and dry rhododendron shrubs.

The condolence photo hounded me all the way to Kathmandu. I didn't make any friends on the trek back to the city. I didn't find the peace I had chased after to the end of the route, the peace I had searched for in the shadow of glaciers and on the denuded tops of glazed mountains. The city disorientated the mind for the rest of the evening. I didn't join my friends for a night out in Thamel even though one after another kept calling me to a farewell dinner for people I barely knew. Another week passed in a daze, without any assignment to occupy the mind, without the slightest inclination towards anything new. Friends kept pulling me back into their raucous, lively evening games, tethered me to their gossips and arguments, filled my glass to the brim whenever I tried to withdraw into myself.

It was back to picking on nothing, looking for paying gigs and waking up disappointed at the day. Just about then, a friend decided to move across town to a new place in Lazimpat. She asked if I would return the books I had borrowed from her. The copy of *The Idiot* that I had carried with me during my walk in the mountains belonged to her. In it was the clipping I had failed to throw away. I carried the condolence photo to a wedding reception where most of my—our—classmates had gathered.

'You didn't know?' Everybody else seemed to know. How had I missed Sparrow's passing while everybody had heard of his long fight against the disease, been there when he was cremated, said kind words to the widow? Some of my classmates were doctors and had treated him towards the end, indulging his request for morphine to ease him into the twilight of his last days, sitting on his bed to chat with him, keeping him laughing until the very end. I grew silent and stared at my drink as my lips quivered, until someone slapped me on the back and put an arm around my shoulders and dragged me away from the tent to smoke cigarettes in a corner hidden from the groom's elders.

'Why didn't anybody tell me?' I asked. Sparrow never had anybody he could have called a best friend, but if anyone ever came close to being called one, it was me. We had even shared the same desk for our SLC exams, comparing trigonometry sums and copying passages from leaves torn from the economics textbook. A supervisor had found us colluding thus, come screaming at Sparrow, who had turned cold and started to sob uncontrollably. I had stared down the supervisor, and growled in a measured voice, 'You couldn't find anybody else to bully?' The supervisor had been quite taken aback and had stomped out of the classroom. And yet, when time came for Sparrow to die, when Sparrow knew that he was on his deathbed, and had been laughing with all the other boys, he hadn't thought of me.

'You are at a wedding reception, you asshole!' A friend passed me the cigarette that was going around. 'Put that thing away. Get yourself drunk. And then we can ask the bride's friends to dance with us.' The DJ had switched from hip hop to Bollywood numbers. Already, pairs of old men were supporting each other's bulk away from the gaze of family and friends to throw up into rose bushes, on another friend's car tyres.

It took me a few days to identify the Chetana that I needed to find. I didn't ask my friends, I didn't go sleuthing on Facebook. I went instead to the newspaper that had published the condolence photo. Since I wrote for the newspaper occasionally, it wasn't difficult to convince the boy in Accounts to show me the phone number of the person who had paid for the photo. The receipt also included an address for a Chetana S. Not an accurate address—

there is no such thing in most of Kathmandu—but the name of the neighbourhood and the street where Chetana lived. Over the next few days, I sat in the recesses of a momo shop and watched her come home from work, sometime after six in the evening, and disappear down an alley. It must be because she was so close to her home that she would walk in a sure and unhurried pace, ducking into the alley without needing to look up even if she were sending a text message from her phone, or already searching for something inside her tote bag. One evening, I approached her from the opposite direction, making sure that she had a twenty-metre lead into the alley, and followed her to a house. She was walking up a stoop, her cell phone pinched between ear and shoulder as she tried to open the door. The jacaranda tree in the yard was in full bloom.

A week passed before I had gathered enough courage. She was inside, flitting from one room to another, picking and settling things, laughing—she must have been on the phone, but to my mind obsessed with finding grief, it sounded as if she had gone mad trying to solve a puzzle. I knocked.

Chetana came to the door in a deep green kurti and a man's lungi, damp hair clinging to her throat. She looked at me as if finally discovering another piece in a puzzle. Her lips parted a little and she gasped—she must have gasped, I think. 'Is Niranjan home?' I asked, suddenly choking up at the lie. I could have said any number of things, introduced myself in any manner I wanted, asked her another question from a catalogue of a million questions. Chetana opened the door wide. Somewhere behind her a gas stove hissed and the babble of roiling water echoed through the rooms.

'I was just making some tea,' she said and disappeared into the kitchen. She turned back from the kitchen door. 'I always make more than a cup. Come in, please, come in and sit.' Sparrow grinned from a wall—the same photo with filed teeth, no garland of withered flowers obscuring his smile. Chetana put a cup of tea before me and disappeared once more. She returned with a framed photo.

'This is you.' She pointed to a corner of the crowded photo. A picnic at Thankot, boys all a tangle of arms around shoulders, boys piled atop each other to fit into the frame. Some sixteen years ago, on the verge of moustaches and muscles. Then she said my name. I nodded.

She tilted her head to a side and watched me. I sipped the tea and waited.

'Niranjan talked about you. He always bought the paper on Sundays and read your essays. We'd read them together.' She remembered some of my essays—the one about mangoes growing on garbage piles in the monsoon; about standing above a cliff, wondering how the body would take the fall; about the crows and the ragpicker in Kolkata. She knew about the school years, how everybody called him Sparrow, how Niranjan remembered me as the kindest of the lot.

'Why did you ask if he was home?' she said after returning the photo to its place in the next room. Her phone rang.

She went to the balcony under the jacaranda to answer, came back to sit, and asked, 'Why?'

'I didn't know what else to ask. What you knew. I was—'

'You never came to the hospital when he was there.' She wasn't accusing me. She waited for me to answer. Then she answered her own question. 'He wouldn't talk about you in front of the other boys, but sometimes he would say things to me. He said you wouldn't come. It wasn't in your nature.'

'I didn't know,' I said. 'Sparrow didn't tell me.' Chetana smiled and murmured the name under her breath. She took my empty cup and disappeared into the kitchen.

'Did you bully him in school?' She was at the door, searching me. 'The other boys, they all had stories about school. They made Sparrow laugh, they made me laugh. Some days in the hospital were like picnics.'

'I didn't know,' I said. I should have been there. I had done him harm, and he had known. I hadn't bullied him through those seven years, but I hadn't stood up for him when I could have.

A teacher lost her jewellery box when we were in the seventh grade. She and her two teenage daughters shared the jewellery box stuffed with plastic and faux-pearl earrings. The baubles were fake but the box wasn't: it was carved and inlaid with Tibetan motifs, a family heirloom for the teacher who had abandoned family to raise her two girls away from oppressive patriarchy. Boys from the tenth grade had stolen the box. They had deposited it in a bathroom locker in our

House. Boys from my year had got a whiff of it. They were breaking the lock one afternoon when I walked in.

'Give it to him,' one of them said, handing me the piece of brick with which they were trying to break the lock open. I tried my hand at it. Sparrow walked in. 'What happened?' he said. 'Whose locker is this?'

'Lost my keys,' another boy said. Sparrow looked at the brick in my hand. I shrugged, gave him the brick. He grinned broadly, grabbed the lock, and twisted the aluminium clasp. It broke. 'This is how it is done,' Sparrow said and threw the lock hard on the floor. It splintered and spewed its guts.

A few hours later, the tenth-grade boys rounded us up in a room and beat us. We didn't know anything about the locker or the jewellery box, naturally. But someone had seen Sparrow play with the pieces of the lock, trying to puzzle it together. Sparrow looked at me with teary eyes. I looked away. We were let go, but they kept Sparrow behind. He emerged bruised and crying, but he had said nothing. Who knows what sort of torture he endured that evening? He never said a word about it.

At the House assembly the next morning, the House Master asked three tenth-grade boys to step up and march to the Principal's office. They were suspended for the theft—the teacher's elder daughter had realized that it had been that bunch of boys, her friends, who had stolen the box. Sparrow swore to us and to the other tenth-grade boys that he had said nothing, that it hadn't been him who ratted out the boys who blamed him for the theft of their jewellery box. We believed him.

But after that, something cold and hard settled between Sparrow and the rest of us. He was especially cold towards me—I should have saved him from the hours of torture at the hands of the seniors. I had handed him the brick, I had pushed him into the maelstrom. I had abandoned him.

Over the months and years, like with every other misfortune we visited unto him, Sparrow forgot that night. We stopped our pranks on him and each other. The senior boys who had been suspended returned to the school but kept their distance from Sparrow. No matter how much they beat him, he had kept his silence, never once betraying a name, never once taking the blame. That sort of thing earns you respect. But I had never forgotten. I hadn't stolen the box—not from the teacher, not from the tenth graders, but I had invited Sparrow to make the theft possible. I could have spared him the beating if I had come clean about the other boys who had recruited Sparrow and me to break the lock.

How much of this did Chetana know, I wondered. How had she met Sparrow? How had he courted her? Or had she courted him, he of the meek disposition, teasing out the packets of hurt and betrayal that he had collected through his school years that quieted his voice and rotted his trust of others?

'I'm heading out in a bit,' Chetana said.

'I should go, too,' I said. Chetana disappeared into a

room and called, 'No, stay a while. You're visiting us for the first time.' She came out wearing the same kurti over turquoise leggings. She smiled as she cleared the table.

The week passed in agony. I didn't know why I obsessed over Chetana as much as I did, I didn't understand what part of myself I wanted to give to her. Over and over, I recited the lines that I was convinced she had written for Sparrow: 'Holding a pear to his chest, begging his wife Chetana to hold his hand, Niranjan died...' It was pointless to try to work. The brain refused to switch off at night; the floor between reality and the quicksand hell of nightmares began to dissolve, so that I'd fall asleep at nine in the morning and wake at four in the afternoon, too weak to do anything but reach for the bottle of water by the bedside. At last, the need to relieve the bladder would force the body out of bed and push it to the bathroom. Hunger would daze and dull the senses, until another set of nightmares put the fear of death in me, and I'd finally stumble to the nearest bhatti where I'd try to eat some meat and drink a glass of raksi. The raksi would go straight to the head and make me morose all over again. All the while, I would think of Chetana, her shapely but widowed legs, the pear and hands she wrote into her husband's condolence notice, the unvanquished light in her eyes.

But I met another friend from school on a Friday morning

and we got to drinking and talking. I didn't mention to him anything about Sparrow or Chetana. He took one look at me and guessed I hadn't been eating for some time. He forced me to eat and made me laugh after we'd had a few rounds of raksi. By the time he left I'd gathered enough energy to want to walk, to wander and take in the sights. By evening, I had wandered all the way to the momo shop near Chetana's apartment in Lazimpat.

She hurried home that evening, but rushed right out, just as I was trying to decide if I should walk up to her door. I lost her by the time I followed her to the main road. She could have gone anywhere. I didn't return the next day, but on Sunday evening I was back in the shop. Chetana didn't return from work so I walked past her apartment after dark. She was home—there was light in the kitchen. On Monday, she wore a pale jacket with canary yellow trousers. On Tuesday, she walked moodily, staring at her feet, swinging her handbag a little. On Wednesday, she rushed home, but unlike on Friday, she didn't come out. Nobody visited her either; at least not from the momo-shop end of her alley. On Thursday, when I reached the momo shop, she was in the corner where I always sat. From the way she tracked my eyes as I walked to her and how she shifted a little on the bench, I knew that she had been waiting for me.

'Why are you doing this?' she asked.

'I don't know,' I said. I became quiet. She asked me questions, answered most of them, half to reassure herself and half to get me to agree with her. 'I feel like there is a part of myself that I have been carrying around, but which really belongs to you,' I said. 'I feel like I owe you something, but I don't know what it is.'

'You miss him. I understand that. I miss him, too,' Chetana said quietly. The owner of the shop had told Chetana about me, and there were a few other regulars at the other tables. I burned with shame. I couldn't meet Chetana's eyes, and I couldn't meet the eyes of anybody else in the momo shop.

'I saw him,' I said, finally gathering the courage to look at her. 'I saw Sparrow in the mountains. I read your words. I've been unsettled ever since.'

She didn't ask me where I had seen Sparrow. She had seen his cremation. Perhaps she had held his still-warm ashes in her hands. Of course she didn't ask me where I had seen Sparrow. I described to her the private shrine to Sparrow her words had created in a tea-lodge high up in the himals.

'Take me there,' she said. 'Take me there.'

We sat in silence for a while until even the silence became something the other people in the momo shop stared at with suspicion. I followed her out to the alley, but didn't follow her into it—I knew we were being watched. 'Take me there, please,' Chetana said.

'I don't have the courage,' I said. She walked away.

⌒♫⌒

I felt better over the next week. I wrote the outlines for a movie and gave it to a director who said he would find a producer to pay for the screenplay. There was a woman, a casual acquaintance, who let me walk her home after a birthday party. I tried to cut back on the drinking and the drifting, and made admirable progress by the end of the week. Over three separate days I wrote three poems and shot them off for publication in local newspapers. Buoyed by successes on these disparate fronts, I called Chetana to invite her for a coffee in Thamel, or perhaps to meet my friends.

She didn't answer her phone until late at night when she called me back. 'I am not in town,' she said. 'I decided to walk to Niranjan. I'll get there in three days.' I told her that I was sorry, that I wished I'd been the one who accompanied her to the tea-lodge where Sparrow waited. She asked me which room I had stayed in. I didn't quite remember at first, but then I remembered which way the windows faced. Chetana thanked me repeatedly. 'I understand what you meant when you said you owed me a part of yourself,' she said. 'I feel the weight of it. I am carrying it with me, taking it to him. Thank you for showing me the way here.'

I didn't think much of the conversation. My friends had invited me out to a house party in Budhanilkantha, in the northern foothills of the Kathmandu Valley. There were new people to talk to and to repeat to them rehearsed platitudes about the personal past and the future. I managed to keep myself sober right to the end of the evening. The next morning felt like a new start. And, soon, Sparrow and Chetana left me. I no longer thought of the guilt and nausea that I had felt in the mountains after seeing Sparrow, or after reading Chetana's words.

Chetana called after about a month. 'Come over tonight,' she said. I was still thinking of an excuse not to go when she told me not to make any excuses and hung up before I could say anything. The momo-shop owner happened to be standing outside the shop when I walked past. He sucked meat out of his teeth and spat it out along with a toothpick, but he didn't look at me with contempt, even though our eyes met. Chetana's apartment, the stoop, and the small yard outside were lit up with lanterns. There were voices inside. She had guests. Knowing that deflated me a little, but I scolded myself. Who was I to expect to be her only guest? But the bottle of wine in the paper bag suddenly felt weighted with foolishness.

A broad-faced man opened the door. More than a dozen unfamiliar faces crowded her small kitchen. More unfamiliar faces spilled over onto the yard. Chetana waved to me from a corner, but she continued talking to a small woman with brightly dyed hair even as she weaved her way through the crowd to hug me. Her breath was liquor-spiced, her eyes a little glazed. 'Let me introduce you to my friends,' she said, but when she turned around, there were just too many of them, and she didn't know where to start. Her friends burst into laughter, as did she, and she pushed me into the crowd, saying, 'You can introduce yourself, can't you?'

Our eyes met through the evening, but we were always in different corners of the house or the yard, mid-conversation with somebody. Most of the people at the party were Chetana's colleagues and friends from work. I was among the very few of her 'civilian' friends, as she put it. She was leaving town, and this was a farewell.

The broad-faced man who'd opened the door for me sidled up and smiled. 'You are Santosh, aren't you?' he asked. I asked how he knew. 'Easy,' he said, 'you're the only person here I don't know.'

'You did a good thing by sending Chetana to that lodge, buddy,' he said. Buddy. I'd barely met the man, but he spoke as if he knew me. 'Chetana told me about you...about you and Niranjan.'

'How do you know Niranjan?'

'I don't,' he said. I finished what was left of my beer. 'Chetana told me about him. I met her on the trail.' He nodded and said, 'We met the second day of our walk. I happened to be going just where she was going. We talked along the way. I knew her story by the time we reached the tea-lodge. She said she needed to stay behind. I know it sounds strange. But I couldn't walk away. I waited for her.'

Chetana hurried to our corner, a dazzling new light brightening her face. 'Oh, you two met,' she said, before someone pulled her away to another, louder corner. The

corner where I and Chetana's trekking companion talked
was the only corner with a bit of sobriety and gravity.
Without us, the evening would have floated loose, climbed
to the ether and dissipated. The man waited for the quiet
to return.

'She seemed lost when I first met her. Literally, because
she had lost her way and wandered nearly a kilometre
towards another village, off the trail. But also in spirit; and
I saw that right away. She was standing at the edge of the
trail, not looking down at the sheer drop or the blue-grey
river at the bottom of the gorge, but at the himals across.
But she wasn't seeing them. I know she wasn't. I had to very
quietly walk up to her and grab her elbow before I asked
her if she was all right.

'When she told me where she was headed I knew she'd
lost her way. I showed her the map and said she'd better
walk with my group. She didn't talk much the first few
days, but I managed to get her to talk.' He grinned at me,
perhaps expecting praise.

'She told me all about Niranjan; how they met, how they
loved and married, and how he died young. But she didn't
mention you, not until the afternoon when we approached
the tea-lodge with the room where she said Niranjan waited
for her. Niranjan had talked of you as his best friend, but
also as his worst bully. I know that isn't how you think of
him. Chetana said you sought her out after you saw the
room with Niranjan's pictures. She said, Santosh is probably
the closest thing to a brother that Niranjan ever had.

'When we reached the tea lodge she asked to be shown that room. She said she didn't want to stay there, but by the evening she'd changed her mind. I left the next day, left her behind and went on to finish the trek. When I came back after three days, she was still there. She said she needed to stay on until she knew that she could leave the place. Leave him, I suppose. I didn't tell her, but I took a room in the lodge next door and waited for her. After three days she came outdoors, saw me smoking outside my lodge and walked over. She just sat there for a while and went back.

'She stayed there for about a week. She asked me to help her find a lama. Then she asked the owner of the lodge if she could strip down the newspapers with Niranjan's pictures. The man didn't want that, he said he'd spent money hauling in the paper and pasting it on the walls. But when the old lama came, he straightaway went into the room where Chetana had been staying. Then he scolded the owner, who had never actually stepped foot into the room. When he saw Niranjan's pictures, he helped her strip the pictures down, as carefully as they could. The old lama asked them to cut Niranjan out of the papers and save him.

He wanted you to come here to let him go, the old lama had told Chetana before ritually burning the pictures as a line of lamas chanted sutras from the *Book of the Dead*.

I thought of the many times I had carried Sparrow's bed out of the dormitory room into the cold air of the night, crossing thresholds of trust, friendship and cruelty. Even in the years when he withdrew from me, there had always been an unseverable bond between us. That bond had dissolved after we went our separate ways and lost touch with each other. I had walked out on him, neglected his need for my presence in his life. I had reverted to thinking of him as the weakling, the defenceless boy that everybody was free to pick on, bully, abuse, discard. But he hadn't forgotten me. He had laid his ambush high up in the mountains and waited for me to stumble into his trap and run wounded towards Chetana, so that I would also lose her.

Chetana crossed the lawn to come and stand by my side. Her friend walked away, giving us the privacy he perhaps thought we wanted. Chetana smiled and sipped her drink, but she didn't say anything. I thought I had nothing to say to her, but I found a welter of emotions rise without the words to build them into decipherable signs. She squeezed my arm and walked away. I looked for her after standing alone for the next ten minutes, checking the time to see when I could quietly slip out of the party. Her friend was at the kitchen sink—wearing a fantastically domestic apron—washing and drying cups for more people who poured in. He gave me a knowing smile, as if he knew me better that I knew him. I turned away to continue searching for Chetana.

ACKNOWLEDGEMENTS

This book is dedicated to my parents; to my friends and teachers at Budhanilkantha and Whitman; to Monika Acharya, Raxak Mahat, and Sarahana Shrestha—for your encouragement; to Sushrut, Tuan, and Mithilesh—you are in these stories;

to Rabi Thapa, Pranab M. Singh, Prachanda M. Shrestha, Sujan Chitrakar and Nayan P. Sindhuliya;

to Suvani Singh—you are the rock, and you are the star;

to Soham Dhakal—for all the laughter and the crazy stories we cook up;

to Bhaskar Dhungana—for never being satisfied with my first attempts;

to the community of writers, poets, and artists in Kathmandu—for the vitality and ambition.

www.ingramcontent.com/pod-product-compliance
Lightning Source LLC
Chambersburg PA
CBHW022141060526
44654CB00043B/622